SOULS INVERTED

a novel

by

William Dele Watson

Copyright © by William Dele Watson 2020

2332 43rd Avenue South

Grand Forks, ND 58201

701-746-9104

1

CHAPTER 1 Enroute to An Khe

Infantry First Lieutenant John Leland Davis threw his duffel bag into the cargo compartment of the UH-1 Huey helicopter. He climbed aboard and fastened the seatbelt in the jump seat behind the pilots. He believes he can get a better view of the terrain from up front. After all, this place will be home for the next 12 months.

Lt. Davis is lucky in that the helicopter on which he hitched a ride to his new home at An Khe was empty except for the crew, which included the crew chief and the gunner each sitting behind their M 60 machine guns in the rear wells of the helicopter, each keeping watch for anything unusual. Further, and even better is the fact that the helicopter belongs to his new unit – the First Cavalry Division. The helicopter was from the 229the Aviation Battalion (Assault Helicopter) of the 1st Cav. He would not have to catch hops to get to An Khe, the division headquarters. He had hooked up with a direct flight.

When flying up the coast northbound toward Qui Nhon the pilots flew about a quarter mile off shore, just outside the surf line. This was known as being "Feet Wet" and stopped any enemy taking potshots at them with small arms fire. Just north of Qui Nhon the pilots changed course nearly directly westbound toward An Khe. They flew above the QL 19 highway which passed An Khe on its way to Pleiku. Since AK 47 rounds were generally almost spent when they reached a straight up altitude of 1,500 feet it was customary to stay above that altitude when over land, except for tactical reasons or landing and taking off. From the ground up to 1,500 feet was known as the "zap zone" which new pilots were taught to avoid. In this case the pilots climbed up to 2,500 feet for an extra buffer.

Looking South back toward Qui Nhon – just before turning west on QL19

Finding out that the new Lieutenant who they informally called "L-T" (El-Tee) was going to the First Cav division they begin to explain the terrain and landmarks in an attempt to orient the new LT to the countryside. One never knew where the 1st Cav would work next week. As of right now, much of the division was in the central highlands near the Cambodian border searching the Ia Drang valley for the 66th, 33rd and 32nd North Vietnamese Regular Army Regiments. It was November 1965 and the 1st Cav would soon find them at LZ X-ray on the Ia Drang river next to Chu Pong mountain (Hill 542).

Warrant Officer 1 (WO1) Edward Grosnos the 19-year-old Pilot in Command (PC) explained to Lt. Davis that there were three levels of Vietnam between them and the Cambodian border. They were currently over the coastal plain which yielded about 10 kilometers inland to a midlevel plateau that ended at An Khe, where the final climb to the central highlands began. The highlands contained mountains of the Annamite chain ranging up to 6,000 feet in height and heavy triple canopy forests. The Chu Pong ridgeline and mountain were included in the central highlands mountains. Most of the level ground was put to use for growing rice.

Looking West through the Mang Yang pass leading to the Central Highlands.

As they flew westbound along QL 19 the final step-up to the central highlands became visible in the distance. The volcanic red QL 19 twisted and turned in switchbacks as it traversed the raising terrain.

"LT, you see where the road goes up the hill?" said Grosnos

"Yes"

"Well, that is the Mang Yang Pass. It is a perfect place for ambushing slow moving military trucks and other vehicles. It's been that way since the French were here. They had a mobile strike force called Groupement Mobile 100 of about 2,500 men ambushed there. Many are buried on the north side of the pass. You can see where the ground is sunken over the gravesites when you fly right over the top. But we aren't going that far, because if you look to the right of the pass you will behold your new home of An Khe."

An Khe refueling area. Copters refueled "hot" in RVN - they did not shut off the engine.

Lt. Davis said nothing, but he already knew the fate of the French mobile strike group, as at West Point he had read Bernard Fall's book *Street Without Joy* in which the loss of the group was covered in detail in Chapter 9, End of a Task Force.[1] But he was sitting up high in his seat and

---

[1] Gen. William C. Westmoreland, the United States commander in Vietnam from 1964 to 1968 kept a copy of Fall's book on the table near his bed. He later said that the defeat of Groupement Mobile 100 was "always on my mind," particularly so during the early U.S. developments. See Mounted Combat in Vietnam by Gen. Donn A. Starry, Department of the Army, Washington DC 1978, page 5, footnote 1.

straining to see what was once history in a book and now a field of battle he might have to fight upon again.

In fact, the 1ˢᵗ Cav's primary mission upon landing in Vietnam that summer was to ensure that QL 19 remained open all the way from Qui Nhon to Pleiku and that the country could not be split in two along the roadway by the North Vietnamese Army. A small U.S. Army Special Forces camp at An Khe had been overrun in February and it was that location chosen by General Kinnard to station the thousands of incoming men and hundreds of machines.[2] The location would eventually have a 19 kilometer perimeter. The helicopter parking area was known as the "golf course" because Brigadier General Wright tried to leave as much grass as possible to keep the dust down during helicopter hovering operations while hand clearing trees and other foliage (bulldozers would have disturbed the grass and top soil and created blinding "brownouts" for the pilots). The official name of the Division Headquarters at An Khe was Camp Radcliff, but that name was rarely used.

Lt. Davis had set back in his seat and relaxed as he now enjoyed the view. Something caught his eye off the left side of the aircraft. Green tracers the size of golf balls were streaming up toward the aircraft. At the same

---

[2] USAMHI, *Senior Officers Oral History Program*, Interview of LTG Kinnard by LTC Jacob B. Couch, Jr., 1983.

instant the Crew Chief in the left well, Sergeant Jake Becker said, "We're taking fire from 9 O'clock. Big stuff like 12.7." He opened up with his M 60 machine gun, but at this distance it was not likely to reach the big gun.

The big rounds began to pound into the aircraft and Lt. Davis watched as pieces of insulation were ripped lose and floated in the air. Then there was silence as the engine quit running.

WO1 Grosnos stayed on the controls and attempted to set up a glide while the copilot switched the radio to the guard frequency, "Mayday, Mayday, Mayday, Tiger 22 on guard, flameout, going down one-five klicks east of An Khe on QL 19. Mayday Tiger 22 shot down one-five klicks east of An Khe heavy machine gun fire."[3]

"Aircraft in distress this is King 26 on guard- state type aircraft, unit and number of souls on board."

"Roger, Tiger 22 is a single UH-1 from the 229th Aviation Battalion, First Cav. We have five souls on board. No need to hurry, we've got damage to the flight controls – aircraft is not responding and we are now rolling inverted. It looks like we'll impact that way."

---

[3] The Ultra High Frequency (UHF) radios in all the military aircraft in Vietnam would monitor (or "guard") the emergency frequency of 243.0 in addition to the current frequency dialed up and being used by the aircraft to communicate. In order to broadcast on guard a large switch could be flipped that automatically tuned the radio to 243.0. King 26 was an Air Force command and control aircraft at high altitude, allowing it to hear many distress calls over a large area.

"Roger that Tiger 22, good luck and call when down safe."[4]

Tiger 22 hit the ground completely upside down at 140 knots. All aboard were killed.

It is important to note here that all of the crew knew that they were going to die within the next 30 seconds, yet there was no change of tone of voice on the intercom or during radio transmissions. This was not the infantry, where adrenaline allowed men to kill with fury and perhaps survive the battle themselves by shear aggression. Among the aircrew there was no need to encourage your troops to carry-on the attack up the hill to victory. No need the stir the adrenaline to fight on. In fact, it was quite the opposite- if they were to survive at all, only calm, reasoned decisions would decide the matter.

They had spent 9 months and 200 flight hours at Fort Wolters, Texas and Fort Rucker, Alabama being trained to stay calm in the aircraft in the event of an emergency. All of their instructors had recently been in Vietnam and would return there after about a year of teaching new students. (It is certain, however that when the microphone was not keyed and when none of the

---

[4] The 39th Rescue Squadron, today an Air Force Reserve Command unit of the 920th Rescue Wing (920 RQW) at Patrick Air Force Base, Florida, used the call sign "King" in Vietnam.

others could hear them, there was a variety of cursing concerning their fate.)

No amount of fearless aggression was going to stop the aircraft from impacting the ground at over 100 g's. Everyone knew and everyone accepted the fact. Many times in the past the ability to instantaneously accept the unbelievable had saved them- engines shot out, fires from severed fuel lines and even flack bursts next to the aircraft may not be fatal- so long as the crew could keep their head and keep adjusting. However, this time there was no way out.

CHAPTER 2 Death on the Doorstep

At 6:00 PM on Sunday, the doorbell rang at the Davis house on Reynolds Drive in Torrance, California. Mrs. Laura Davis put down her dish towel and walked toward the doorway.

It seems strange or even cruel, looking back on the events of the mid-1960's that the United States Army would not have sent a Chaplin to inform the family of the death of their loved one, but in 1965 the build-up of troops in Vietnam was just beginning and the tens of thousands of American young men who would eventually die there could not be foreseen or even envisioned. Death notifications were sent out telegram.[5]

She opened the door and the messenger announced that he had a telegram for Mr. & Mrs. Davis and then without waiting he placed it in her hand, turned and left the porch. No matter that there was no Chaplin, Mrs. Davis had waited for her husband during World War II while he flew 35 missions on a B17 as a radio operator. She knew what a telegram to a serviceman's family meant. Laura was frozen with fear and the envelope fell to the floor through her immobile fingers. She heard a terrible scream, the howl of a wounded animal in horrible

---

[5] See, *We Were Soldiers Once and Young*, H. Moore & J. Galloway, Random House, 1992, page 323, referring to the Battle of the Id Drang in November 1965.

pain. Then she realized that the scream was coming from her.

Jim, her husband, and her son Davy came running to the entrance hallway and momentarily stopped as they saw Laura's contorted face and her hand pointing to the telegram on the floor. Davy supported his mother as her knees buckled and she began to fall.

Jim quickly picked up the telegram, knowing as a WWII veteran that it did not always mean death, but could mean John was wounded or captured. He carefully read:

"The Secretary of Defense asks that I assure you of his deepest sympathy in the loss of your son First Lieutenant John Leland Davis who reports indicate was killed in an air crash on 6 November 1965 in Vietnam. Due to existing conditions Lt. Davis' body cannot be returned at present. Confirming letter to follow. Dunlap, Acting Adjutant General"

When he finished reading and looked up with tears streaming down his face, his family already knew they had lost John. They stood in the hallway hugging, crying and holding up Laura. Laura, confused and still in shock repeated several times, "But he only left two weeks ago."

Jim and Davy took Laura to the bedroom and lay her down on the bed. He then went to the phone and called their Priest at Saint Lawrence Martyr Church and asked him to come over as quickly as possible.

Will was away in his first year at the University of California, Berkeley. Jim would later call the university administration and request that Will be contacted and told to call home.

It was another week before a young Captain visited the house and explained to the family that he had been assigned to assist them with the Army processing of funeral arrangements and the return of John's body. John would be accompanied by a member of the First Cavalry Division from Vietnam to his final interment. The family had chosen the National Cemetery at Riverside, California for his final resting place.

The local newspaper had printed his obituary and did a human interest story on a local boy who had made the paper before as an outstanding football and track & field athlete in high school- who had been killed-in-action in a far off place most people had never heard of. Many of his neighbors and high school friends filled the church to overflowing for the service.

Because the National Cemetery was over an hour away, the interment was limited to a private family ceremony. A General Officer supervised the removal of the U.S. Flag from the coffin, watched it being folded into a triangle and took it with one white gloved hand below and the other above. He slowly and carefully carried the flag to the spot where Laura Davis sat in a folding chair in a black dress, black hat and veil. He very slowly kneeled and offered the flag to Laura stating, "Please accept this flag on behalf of a grateful nation." Weeping, she took the flag in her black gloved hands and cradled it in her arms as she had once done with her son.

CHAPTER 3 John Stops by Home

Both Will and Davy very much looked up to John. Perhaps part of it was the age difference. John had been conceived before the WWII started, but was born in 1942, after Jim had enlisted in the Army Air Force. Will and Davy were both born after the War. Will in 1947 and Davy in 1949. So there was quite an age difference between John and his two brothers- John was five years older than Will and 7 years older than Davy.

After the war, Jim had used his interest in radios as an operator and went back to school on the GI Bill to obtain a BS in electrical engineering from Michigan State University. Both Jim and Laura were from Lansing Michigan and had met in high school. They stayed with Laura's parents while Jim completed his degree.

In 1951 Jim accepted a job at Douglas Aircraft, Long Beach Division. In the nearby city of Torrance, California, great tracts of houses were being built to accommodate the returning GI's and the exploding aerospace industry of southern California. Jim and Laura bought their house on Reynolds Drive in Torrance.

1950's Torrance was the epitome of what everyone nowadays thinks the 1950's were like. Gunsmoke and Deputy Fife on TV, economy sturdy and work available (although nobody in a tract house in Torrance was well-to-do), crime virtually nonexistent and BBQ's burning charcoal flavored the neighborhood breezes. In Torrance in the mid-1950's the stereotypes were all absolutely true. The family had a happy and full life there.

John was truly a child of the 1950's, graduating from Torrance High School in 1959. His values were almost identical to those of his father. A firm belief in God and country and that through hard work anything was possible. Hard work at academics and athletics made possible his selection to attend West Point.

Jim was so proud of John that he told him so several times when he was home on leave before he left for Vietnam, even though Jim was normally very sparing in praise of his children. Jim felt a father's deep love for his son, especially knowing the peril that awaited him. As John stood in the middle of the living room after arriving and setting his duffle bag on the floor, then hugging his mother and brother, Jim had marveled at this beautiful, trim young officer with the crewcut and bright smile. Jim did not allow himself to admit that he was also proud of himself for having at least a part in creating such a fine young man. He made a silent prayer to God bless his son and to protect him and keep him safe.

Neither Will or Davy were of the 50's generation. Their attitudes were different than John's solid footing with the respect for authority and conformity in social norms.

First, what people call the 60's did not correspond directly to the calendar 1960's. The 60's that people recall in memory today as the crazy period of sex, drugs and rock & roll, draft dodging and attempted revolution was a period from about the mid 1960's to the mid 1970's.

Will had graduated from high school in 1964 and went to U.C. Berkeley. Up until his departure for Berkeley, Will was on the tail end of the 50's generation. However, he was an unusual child for any period in history because he had already decided upon a vocation. He was to be a priest.

Will was an average boy in many respects, he liked sports, especially basketball because he grew to six feet in height by his junior year, but he was not a standout star. His grades were good, but that was because he worked hard, was bright and knew he was not a genius. He had dated, but had not formed any permanent bond with a "girlfriend", although he might have if it had not been so culturally difficult to engage in sexual activity in the early

60's (the ending part of the 50's culture where young women disappeared to visit "relatives" should they become pregnant). He was well liked at school and was a good listener.

What Will did have was an identity crisis. His life was flat- without the effervescence he saw in so many other students who got great joy in everyday events such as the pregame pep rally. But neither was he depressed- it seemed to him that he was just putting in time on earth. He wanted more. To help hundreds, thousands and even millions of people if possible. The thought of helping people made him happy and the thought of helping many gave him great joy.

Will reasoned that of all the beings who have walked upon the earth, the one who had helped many millions of people through their troubled lives was Jesus Christ. The purity of His goodness was unquestioned. Will could devote his life trying to emulate Jesus and be solid and sure he was on the right path. The love and kindness of the savior meant he need hold nothing back. Complete devotion.

As he had grown up Will had held back from believing and following others because people could truly believe they were helping when they were really causing harm. People could also be intentionally evil and cause harm simply to benefit themselves. The newspapers were full of stories of such criminals and con artists. He realized he would never be able to completely trust another human being without critically evaluating their motivations and actions.

However, one could without reservation put all their trust, faith and actions in the service of a perfect God. He had read St. Augustine's *City of God* and believed him when Augustine said that the only true happiness is to know God and carry-out His will for you. All other things in this temporal life on earth are of little consequence.

He wanted to enter the seminary as badly as John had wanted to go to West Point. But before the seminary he needed to get a BS in philosophy and headed off to Berkeley in the fall of 1964.

The Philosophy Department at Berkeley was relatively small in number at that time. One of the first people Will met upon arrival was second year student Mario Savio, who also had plans to become a priest.[6]

---

[6] Mario Savio, 53, Campus Protester Dies, New York Times, By Eric Pace, Nov. 7, 1996. Obituary.

CHAPTER 5 A Dark House

When Will had left for Berkeley, Davy was starting his junior year at South Torrance High School. The school had recently been erected to accommodate the large number of baby boomers populating Torrance at the time. In November, 1965, at the time of John's death Davy was half way through his senior year and had yet to plan past his graduation. But that had changed after John was killed. He now had a plan for his life following graduation.

Davy was without doubt a full-fledged member of the 60's generation. He was tall and thin like Will, but his body was deeply tanned from hours surfing on the beaches of Southern California. His hair was long and a naturally a light brown color, but was blond from long hours on the beach.

Davy had worked in in a supermarket bagging groceries in order the buy an old 1960 Volkswagen van, which would hold his surfboard. Each day he would leave the house at 6:30 in the morning and drive along the beaches between Hermosa and Redondo to find an uncrowded place to surf for an hour before school. Early in the morning, with an off-shore breeze, the waves would not be large, but the ocean would be so calm that one could see through the well-formed curl as if looking through thin glass. He could lose himself in the waves and had to be careful not to be late for school.

He would shower and rinse in the public showers on the beach and dry off as he walked to the VW van. After slipping into his school clothes in the privacy of the rear of the van, he would exit and comb his blond hair in the large side mirror before getting in and driving to school. Every day, even late in the day, Davy looked like he had just gotten out of the shower.

Even if one could not tell by looking at Davy, he was deeply disturbed by the forced changes in his life. Both

John and Will were gone and his mother had changed from the mother bear guarding her cubs to a subdued, sad and unhappy person. Her passion in life and the happiness which once was felt upon entering the house had died or was at least incapable of her at this moment. She went through the motions and kept busy, but there was no spontaneity or joy in her life. A pall of death hung over the house.

Jim too seemed to be on autopilot – get home from work at 5:30 PM. Read the newspaper until supper at 6:00 PM. He would then sit in his recliner and concentrate on the ceiling, or somewhere in the far distance above the ceiling until he turned-in at 10:00 PM. The days were the same.

Davy felt guilty that he could not bring some relief to his mother, who seemed to appreciate his attempts to help around the house and cheer her up- but was still was deeply sad.

He didn't know what to do and decided to talk to his father who he considered the rock of the family and who had shown courage and bravery in battle. It was a good time to do so since his mother was at a church function for the evening.

Jim told him that his mother was a strong person and she would recover, but it was doubtful that anything that Davy could do would speed the process. He told Davy just to keep loving and helping her, but to keep in mind that only time would wear the sharp edge from her loss. He told Davy that the loss of a child for a mother brings on a special kind of grief that one who is not a mother cannot imagine. And John was a good son – all that she or he could ever ask that he be. Davy watched as his father's eyes welled with tears, but he continued speaking to Davy. "It may take years before the mention of John's name brings back fond memories of a beloved son instead of the agony of seeing a telegram on the floor that she had recoiled against and would not accept."

Jim looked up through the ceiling again and, as if thinking out loud said, "You will find as you go through life that the only person you can really count on is your mother. Others, even perhaps your own relatives, will weigh the circumstances before backing you up- but not your mother. The bond between the one who gave you life and you is unbreakable, for as long as you both exist. It is the law of nature- and when that bond is broken by the early death of a child it is unnatural and unbearable."

Davy hesitated, trying to let it all sink in, "OK, thanks Dad, I'll just try to help and give it time". Davy rose and started toward his room. He noted that the house had grown quite dim during their conversation as the winter sun had set. He looked back down the hallway and into the living room. He saw his father still sitting in his chair, head tilted back and still staring upward. Jim did not move to switch on a lamp as the darkness filled the room. Davy now realized that his father was just as filled with heartache as his mother but he had failed to see it because he thought the strength his father had shown throughout his life meant he was indestructible. For the first time in his life he had seen his father as a human being and not as an idealized protector and hero.

Davy closed the door to his bedroom and flipped on the light. He was trying to figure out a way to tell his mother that he wanted to follow in John's footsteps and honor him by joining the Army. In fact, he had already joined the Army on the "delayed entry program" since he was now 18 years old and could, and did, sign up on his own. He would report for duty shortly after high school graduation.[7] His report date was 14 August 1966. Volunteering instead of waiting to be drafted gave him the option of choosing what his job would be in the Army. He had signed up for helicopter pilot training. This enticement offered him by the Army to enlist only entitled

---

[7] If a male over 18 years was not in college he would be given a physical examination and possibly drafted into the service for a period of 2 years. The odds of being called were greatly increased after the 1965 Vietnam troop build-up. A draftee would serve where the Army needed him, regardless of the individual's personal preference. This often meant that draftees ended up in the infantry. Some liked it – most not.

him to get to the flying school. After that he would be on his own – to earn his wings or wash out.

He picked up his books to start his homework when the explosion went off. He threw open his door and ran to the living room where he saw his dad still staring at the ceiling, but with lifeless eyes. A 1911 Army Colt 45 ACP semi-automatic pistol lay on the floor next to the chair.

Jim had done the full 35 missions in B17's and had seen many boys and young men horribly ripped apart by fighters and flak. But now, in his mind's eye they all looked like John. He simply could not stand the pain of flying his 36th mission over and over, forever. Each time firing the red flare gun from the waist gunner's window just before landing to let the medics and ambulances know of wounded aboard and to hurry to meet them at the end of their landing roll. And each time helplessly watching his own son die before help arrived.

CHAPTER 6 Will Becomes A Warrior

Will had gone up to Berkeley a month before school
started in 1964 in order to complete his registration and
sign into campus dormitory housing. He had spent the

time getting familiar with the campus and the city of Berkeley. He had found out that the city had been named for George Berkeley, an Irish clergyman who had formed a society to study the "new philosophy" of Thomas Locke. Bishop Berkeley came to the colonies to found a new university, but failed in the attempt. However, it seemed to Will that his following of Locke was on the right track as Thomas Jefferson was also one who studied and believed in Locke's teachings regarding individual rights. Locke, along with St. Thomas Aquinas, believed that God had given each human being specific basic "natural rights" that no other human being could take away because they were given by a higher power than simply another man.[8] That remained true even if the humans had organized themselves into governing agencies with the physical powers to enforce "laws" that invaded God's natural laws. Such human laws would be null and void as being in violation of the will and the laws of God.

It didn't take long for Will to encounter student protests on the campus, but he had no idea what they were about. He found that the student "Free Speech Movement" for First Amendment rights of political speech on the campus itself was the prime mover of such events. At the time there were strict rules prohibiting political

---

[8] Generally, these natural "laws" are set forth in the second paragraph of the Declaration of Independence and the first ten Amendments to the United States Constitution (the Bill of Rights).

advocacy and fundraising on campus. He was interested in the protests, but not enough to engage in them. Besides, he was just starting his freshman year and had no extra time to devote to nonacademic activities. However sometimes the demonstrations couldn't be avoided.

On October 1, 1964, Jack Weinberg was sitting at a table near Sproul Hall collecting donations and volunteers to travel to Mississippi to register black voters in the upcoming summer. He refused to show his identification to the campus police and was arrested. There was a spontaneous movement of students to surround the police car in which he was to be transported. The police car remained there for 32 hours, with Weinberg inside it. It was estimated that there were as many as 3,000 students blocking the police car. The car was used as a speaker's podium. Will stood and listened as Mario Savio address the crowd.

Will sought out Savio, who he knew a little by now from their philosophy classes together, and asked why he risked expulsion for demonstrating on campus. Savio replied, "I spent the summer in Mississippi. I witnessed tyranny. I saw groups of men in the minority working their wills over the majority. Then I came back here and found the university preventing us from collecting money for use there and even stopping us from getting people to go to Mississippi to help."[9]

On December 2, 1964 another demonstration was held at Sproul Hall. The demonstration was orderly and students sang folk songs with Joan Baez leading. On the steps of Sproul Hall, Mario Savio gave a speech:

"This is a firm, and if the Board of Regents are the board of directors, ... then the faculty are a bunch of employees and we are the raw material. But we're a bunch of raw material that don't mean to be made into any product! Don't mean to end up being bought by some clients of the university, be they the government, be they industry, be they organized labor, be they anyone! We're human beings! ... There's a time when the operation of the machine becomes so odious — makes you so sick at heart — that you can't take part. You can't even passively take part. And you've got to put your bodies upon the gears and upon the wheels, upon the levers, upon all the apparatus, and you've got to make it stop. And you've got to indicate to the people who run it, to the people who own it, that unless you're free, the machine will be prevented from working at all."

Will listened carefully to Savio's speech and was mesmerized by its message, "...You can't even passively take part. And you've got to put your bodies upon the gears and upon the wheels, upon the levers, upon all the

[9] Mario Savio, 53, Campus Protester Dies, New York Times, By Eric Pace, Nov. 7, 1996. Obituary.

apparatus, and you've got to make it stop." What Will took from the speech was that Jesus Christ himself had let his body be put upon the gears and wheels to make us all free. He was stunned. Mario Savio was not only saying that one may worship Christ, but that when necessary one had to step up and suffer death on the cross as did Jesus. Jesus had said "enough" to the powers of evil here on earth. We may be called upon to do the same. Those who stopped Blacks in the South from registering to vote were evil. So were those administrators at Berkeley who supported the evil ones in Mississippi by stopping the fundraising for an active opposition to voter suppression in the South.

These early student protests were, for the most part, without injury or property destruction. They were modeled on the Civil Rights Movement led by Dr. Martin Luther King and others who believed the best way to succeed in securing full minority rights was through nonviolent civil disobedience. Of course, Will knew nothing of such things, but on-the-spot he decided he would not stand idle while such injustices existed in the world. If he needed to be a martyr in the cause of righteousness by throwing his body upon the gears, he would do so. And if he were called upon to do more to oppose the evil perpetrated against man by men, he would be St. Michael and Captain the army of God.

Thus was born, in his nineteenth year, the future fourth most wanted man on the FBI's 10 Most Wanted List.

CHAPTER 7 Davy Learns to Fly

August 14, 1966 was approaching for Davy. He couldn't change that. Technically he was already a soldier in the U.S. Army simply awaiting his departure. As terrible as things had been he was at least glad that his mother's parents had agreed to move from Lansing to the house in Torrance so that his mother could look after them in their senior years. They were already in their mid-seventies and slowing down somewhat. But even more than their care he was glad his mother had company and a new mission that gave her a purpose in life. She had even become more devout in her churchgoing and seemed to have some kind of divine fortitude- she never complained, but Davy knew it could not have been easy for her.

On the 14th of August, Davy took a bus to the military L.A. Induction Station at 1033 S. Broadway in downtown Los Angeles where he signed a few more papers and was put right back on a bus to LAX (near where he lived). His package of documents contained an airline ticket to Houston, Texas and instructions to board a military bus for his final destination of Fort Polk, LA.

Upon arrival at Fort Polk Davy was surprised when the busload of new trainees were simply told to take their belongings into a barracks building and find a bunk. There was no yelling and screaming or harassment. He found that this first stop was at the "Reception Center". It was here that they would undergo further processing and be assigned to a basic training company. The processing included a buzz cut hair cut and the issue of uniforms and equipment to be used during their training.

Fort Polk is a beautiful wooded area in Louisiana not far from Alexandria. The Post was a typical WWII camp with white wood frame two-story buildings designed to house one platoon (about 40 soldiers) each. Davy was assigned to a basic training company of approximately 120 soldiers who were destined for many different military specialties in the Army. No matter what your specialty, the several months long basic training was required of all entering soldiers. Thereafter those who were going to special schools such as Davy and any other soldiers bound for specific training would leave Fort Polk. Those soldiers designated for infantry training would remain for "Advanced Individual Training" in infantry tactics in "Tiger Land". It was said that those who washed out of flight school were sent right back to attend Tiger Land and shipped to Vietnam. Nobody knew if that was true or not, but it was not unbelievable and therefore considered by all the budding pilot candidates.

Davy found that the days were long, filled with running in formation, shooting at the rifle range and calisthenics. None of these presented any special problems for him. In August of course the temperature and humidity were both high, but livable. He found that the Drill Sergeants were sane and stable (unlike their normal presentment in the movies) and if you did as instructed one could complete the entire course with a minimum of fuss. The only problem he encountered were blisters. The Army issued well-constructed heavy leather boots that were indestructible, but very difficult to break-in. Running shoes were not issued or perhaps did not yet exist. At any rate, his feet were a bloody mess for the first month.

Fort Polk Infantry Advanced Individual Training (AIT) 1968

Following graduation he and several other of the members of the company scheduled for flight school were put on an olive drab (OD) color bus and shipped to Fort Wolters, Texas. They went west from Louisiana to Dallas and continued west from Fort Worth and then north to Mineral Wells, where the U.S. Army Primary Helicopter School was located.

Flight students spent 4 months here learning the basics of helicopter flying, but only three months were

41

actually spent flying the helicopter. The enlisted warrant officer "candidates" (the old Army Air Corps had called them "cadets", but they were the same lot) the first month consisted of a warrant officer OCS (officer candidate school). Days and nights were filled with Tactical Officers (TACS) yelling in their faces and giving orders for impossible tasks. The TAC Officers worked in shifts so that day or night they were always present. There was very little sleep and hundreds of inspections of every description. A TAC Officer finding a thread on a uniform or a dirty razor would issue "demerits". If the weekly total of the demerits exceeded the maximum allowable, the candidate would be dismissed from the program. The stress was on purpose and designed to edit out those who couldn't take it or didn't want to put up with it. All the while, the TAC Officers would stand candidates at attention and yell in their ear from three inches away that, "You should quit now candidate, you will never make it through this program. Just say you quit and you can get a cold beer and a good night's sleep- go ahead and just tell me you quit."

There were a few that quit and a few that were eliminated, but most survived the harassment and moved on to the next phase of training. Besides, most really wanted to fly and all remembered Tiger Land.

Davy knew what a sergeant and a lieutenant (a commissioned officer) were because he had seen them as leaders in his basic training company, but he had no idea of what a "warrant officer" (WO) was, although with any luck he would become one. It was explained to him that warrant officers were specialist officer experts in their field who rank below a lieutenant and above a sergeant. Many of the Army helicopter pilots were WO's. Warrant Officers were not required to be college educated and generally did not command troops except their own crewmembers when airborne. The warrant officers were the "line pilots" for the Army, staying in the cockpit while their commissioned officer pilot leaders usually left the cockpit above the rank of captain to serve in positions of higher responsibility.

There were some basic helicopter classes during the first four weeks so that the candidates would have some idea of how a helicopter works before they actually climbed into one. Davy was surprised how simple in theory the whole thing worked. The main rotor blows air down just like a ceiling fan – this action causes a reaction against the ceiling except the ceiling is much stronger than the reaction against it and does not move. When the main rotor of a helicopter blows a huge volume of air down, the upward reaction against the rotor blades is enough to lift the whole helicopter off the ground. The amount of air blown downward depends on the pitch angle (bite) of each blade as it travels around the circle. The angle of the blades is controlled by the pilot – pull up on the horizontal rod (the "collective pitch") located to the left of his seat and the helicopter goes up, push down and the helicopter goes down. At the end of the collective pitch rod is a twist grip throttle of the type used on motorcycles and is used to keep the main rotor turning at a constant speed (RPM).

There was also a stick perpendicular to the floor between the pilot's legs like people are used to seeing in airplanes (the "cyclic stick"). It tilts the rotor system (and therefore the helicopter itself) so the pilot may bank (turn) the aircraft and adjust the nose up or down to set the airspeed. There are foot pedals connected to a small rotor at the rear of the aircraft so that the pilot can control the direction of the nose of the aircraft and are usually for use while at a hover.

Although it did not look complicated Davy had not contemplated that both arms and both legs had to move the controls at the same time in coordination with each other to actually make the machine fly under control. He was to find out that it was more like riding a bicycle than studying a book. You could read every book written about how to ride a bicycle and still not be able to ride the bike the first time you tried. Same with the helicopter, it was all muscle memory and physical learning. The instructors said that given enough time they could teach a monkey to fly a helicopter, but the Army wanted it all done in 9 months and would not spend an unlimited amount of time and money on any one particular student when another draftee awaited in the wings. There were periodic check rides "stage checks" designed to weed out those who were not progressing properly. Sometimes these wayward soldiers were "set back" to repeat the failed phase of their training or they were simply eliminated.

Fort Wolters had three huge heliports where over a hundred small training helicopters were based and 25 outlying small paved training sites called "stage fields". The remote stage fields spread out the density of the training activities, but all the helicopters still had to come home to roost at the end of the day at one of the large heliports. At launch and recovery, the air was thick with aircraft and several midair collisions occurred during Davy's time there.

The first time Davy strapped-in to the TH-55 (Hughes 269) small training helicopter he watched his instructor as he expertly lifted the craft and moved over to the center of a large field and brought it to a perfectly still 3 foot hover. His instructor said, "I am going to give you one control at a time so you can feel it and then I will give you all the controls at the same time and ask that you hover over this spot without moving. OK, you have the cyclic stick." Davy held the stick and tried not to move it at all, but the aircraft started swinging from side to side in a pendulum like fashion, each larger than the next. The instructor said, "OK I have the controls". The collective pitch and the trail rotors pedals were each given to his control in turn.

The instructor said, "OK now I'm going to give you all the controls and I still want you to continue to hover over this spot." Davy took the controls and within 15 seconds was swinging from one edge of the field to the other, at times looking directly down at the ground through his side door. He was radically overcontrolling and was sure they would crash unless the instructor immediately rescued them. He looked over to his instructor to save them and saw the instructor was laughing hysterically and enjoying himself immensely. If it had not been for his shoulder straps Davy was sure that the instructor would have been doubled over with laughter.

Finally, the instructor took the controls and called the tower for departure from the stage field. He said, "Don't worry, nobody can hover the first day. We don't really practice it for over a few minutes because it really can't be taught right off the bat. It will come naturally to you in a few hours. But we do a lot of airwork. OK you have the controls – just fly along straight and level and make some turns if you like – get the feel of the aircraft. But when you turn the aircraft, I want to see your head turn that direction first to clear us – this is a crowded place". Davy was quite relieved that once in forward flight the aircraft was stable and he was able to at least keep it upright and control it.

After a few hours Davy loved flying the helicopter. He especially loved doing the gliding emergency landings following the simulated engine failures that were practiced on nearly every flight. The aircraft would only glide (autorotate) if the collective pitch rod was quickly lowered following the engine failure. Failure to lower the collective pitch was certain death as the blades would not windmill if left at a high pitch angle – they would stop and the aircraft will fall literally like a rock. At the bottom of the glide the aircraft was flared to slow it down and then the last burst of lift from the rotor system was used to cushion the landing. Many times these simulated engine failures were given as a surprise. Davy learned to always be aware of potential landing sites along the flight path and to get the collective pitch down without delay. Accept your emergency immediately and do not enter into denial – you cannot wish it away.   Don't get frozen and don't get excited. The natural reaction for an untrained person is one of surprise, shock or disbelief, which is called the "startle effect". The brain absorbs "scary" information and registers fear before we are even consciously aware of it. This reaction can be trained out of most humans by repetition and immediately reverting to a well learned set of predetermined steps that become muscle memory. In fact, Davy would have thought it odd NOT to have been given a surprise simulated engine failure and forced landing on a dual training flight. The instructors said to just do the best you can with the circumstances you are encountering. Even if you are going to crash, lock your shoulder harness and fly the aircraft all the way through the crash sequence. It was constantly drilled into all the students that the question is not if the engine will fail, but that it will fail and you must be ready – and where they were going after training the cause of the engine failure will probably be an AK47 round.

Davy soloed at 13 hours in the aircraft and even surprised himself that he was able to hold the aircraft at a rock steady hover without any conscious effort at all on his part. He just willed the aircraft to hover and it did. He had never really "learned" how to hover – his ability to do it just happened. The training wheels were off and he was now ready to go to Fort Rucker, Alabama to fly the UH-1 Huey.

Each week on Saturday night a USO bus arrived at one of the large buildings on Fort Wolters. The bus was full of girls from Texas Woman's University in Denton, Texas. It was a wonderful thing for these young ladies to do and very much appreciated by the young GI's who were far from home and sometimes lonely. The soldiers were lined up and as each girl exited the bus she would be joined by the next GI in the line who would be her date for the evening.

Davy stepped forward from the line and stepping down from the bus was the most beautiful girl he had ever seen. She was tall with red hair and freckles and sparkling green eyes. Her name was Alice O'Reilly and she was as Irish as a 4 leaf clover. She was a third-year nursing student at the college in Denton. At the end of the evening she gave him her permanent home address in Houston so that they could correspond since Davy was leaving for Fort Rucker. Davy never felt better in his life.

Will didn't drink or use drugs but he found Berkeley to be intoxicating in its own manner. Vigorous discussions in a multitude of cafes and private homes were filled passionate discussions by liberals, socialists, Marxists, and "Old Left" 1930's communists. Will fell in with many of these groups and became enamored by those who called themselves the "New Left". He spent less and less time on his school studies as his time with his new friends increased.

Will learned that the "New Left" felt that "Old Left" communists who supported the Soviet Union of the Stalin era had not followed the true essence of Marxism, which was to restore man to his true state of nature where all property was communal and not "owned" by any private person. If all property is communal, all share in the fruits of their labor. It is the evil of private property which makes possible the exploitation of labor. Stalin killed millions of people in attempting to establish the rural utopia where all farmers 'collectively" owned the land they farmed. Stalin either killed the resisters outright or confiscated their corps after the harvest and left the people there to starve.[10] After Stalin's death even the

---

[10] Stalin said that the death of one man is a disaster for a family that loses its breadwinner, but the death of a million people consisting of entire families is

Soviet Union went through a program of "de-Stalinization."

The New Left felt that Marx was correct but that Stalin had simply botched the experiment. Most of the New Left were committed to a revolution, if necessary, in the United States because they felt the principals upon which the country was founded could not be stretched far enough to set up a true utopian "primitive communism"- fair wealth distribution without a ruling class. Property rights were enshrined in the fundamental founding document of the Constitution in the Fifth Amendment. So a new country from the revolution forward was required- one based upon a new progressive and enlightened constitution without the impediments to socialism presented by the outdated current document.

In the early 1960's many of the Berkeley radicals were looking to Fidel Castro as perhaps the answer to their need for kinder, gentler communist regime. One where the people themselves actually did govern by participatory democracy, meaning through "soviets" that were councils of real workers. However, after his victory Castro ran firing squads 24 hours a day for two weeks, eliminating potential rivals and others. Apparently, Castro was not a believer in the New Left, preferring a style of

---

merely a statistic – there is none left to mourn.

leadership closer to that of Stalin and Mao – a dictator sitting atop a strong and cruel central government. The radicals were disappointed but not discouraged.

Will sat in the coffee shops and learned and debated with the fervor of one whose synapses were all firing-off at the same time. Most of his beliefs were questioned and examined and many were modified or changed. For example, he had always believed true happiness can only come from pursuing God's will for you and then living in accordance with that will as set forth by St. Augustine.

His friend at the table said that Will's concept of the "pursuit of happiness" was put in the Declaration of Independence by Thomas Jefferson, but the concept was around long before Jefferson or even Augustine. It came from the ancient Greeks and not any imaginary God. Just the "pursuit" of happiness (however "happiness" is defined) is enough to give hope that the pursuit will someday be successful.

Socrates said, "Know thyself" meaning you must evaluate yourself as if someone else was conducting the inventory of your conscious and unconscious self. All your strengths and weaknesses, likes and dislikes honestly displayed. This is very hard to do, especially in judging one's faults. Most people lie to themselves about their weaknesses and bad acts as a form of denial for self-survival- they cannot face the truth. Some may never be able to do it. But once you force yourself to face the truth you will know your own genuine nature and a compatible life purpose. Pursuing and achieving this purpose will give you true happiness.

The student continued by stating that Aristotle also stated that true happiness is using those things in human nature for which we are best suited and enjoy. Since it is the power of the human mind and its ability to reason that sets us above the other animals, for Aristotle true happiness for most human beings is a life of contemplation of science and philosophy. Intellectual power and energy is foremost in the nature of humans and therefore its use gives true happiness.

Will drank it all in as the student continued by adding that even if you are still searching for your own ultimate happiness, *the "pursuit" is hope in itself and gives meaning to a person's life.* Without at least the chance of the "pursuit", one has no reason to endure the pain of this physical existence. Without hope of future happiness one welcomes death.

Another student at the table spoke up that religion is the opiate of the masses (the old tired refrain of the Marxists, but new to Will), "The ruling class tells the masses of oppressed people to have faith in God so they don't lose hope and rise up against the ruling class- the oppressors can always say, 'OK, your life is a piece of shit right now, but if you are good and do as you are told here on earth, you will get to a very nice place after you are DEAD.' The bottom line is that there is a confidence game going on and you are the mark. If it sounds too good to be true it probably is – and God is the bogus investment you have to buy into to get your fantastic reward. Do not fall for the con job."

Will was uncomfortable hearing that God was a mental construct of those who were the rich and powerful and yet he could not deny that it was exciting to hear these accusations against all that he had once held holy. He had seen his own mother on her knees praying for hours in church and with her rosary beads and could not imagine that she could have survived the last several years without God. And she was not one of the "oppressed masses"- she was his beloved mother who had lost her son and husband within a very short period. If she had not had some hope of rejoining them in heaven, would she not have done away with herself too? Will still clung to the idea that God was more than just a tool of the ruling class. He had seen otherwise.

"What difference does it make to you anyway", said another student to Will, "You have already accepted the necessity of pushing through to Marxism by violent revolution. The system here allows no other choice. If you must fight or even kill you can do so in the name of God or in the name of the glorious revolution – either way we get the revolution and God can cram the rest up his ass."

One of the other students spoke up, "You better hope that God and his ass are really imaginary otherwise he will probably put out a contract on you with Will as the hit man. I suggest that we concentrate on the revolution and leave the Big Guy out of it altogether". Will replied, "One can kill at God's direction and know it is good and righteous, but if one kills on their own volition there is great possibility of evil. As St. Augustine said, 'There must be a justification for war. Christians need not be ashamed of protecting peace…, but peacefulness in the face of a grave wrong that can only be stopped by violence is a sin. Defense of one's self or others is a necessity."[11]

---

[11] However, Will left out that Augustine held that an individual Christian under the rule of a government engaged in an unjust war has no choice but to subject themselves to their political masters (but should ensure that they execute their war-fighting duty as justly as possible). After all, the purpose of Augustine's book *City of God* was to address claims that the Christian religion was one of the causes of Rome being sacked in 410 by Alaric the Visigoth. Augustine assures the Roman Empire that Christians are good citizens in all respects, including in performing their military duties if called upon by the government. Later, St. Thomas Aquinas also addressed the requirements for a just war in his *Summa Theologica*.

Will opposed the U.S. government's "unjust" war on North Vietnam. By this time, with the huge build-up of U.S. troops in Vietnam, Will felt that violent resistance against the American government was, in itself, a "just war" under God's laws. He had studied the history of Vietnam since WWII and decided that the Supreme Commander of the Allied forces in that theater, Lord Louis Mountbatten was correct in advising French Commander General Leclerc in 1945, "Not to fight but to try and make friends as the British had done in Burma and Malaya... liberate Indochina from the Japanese and give them freedom if that was what they would like. This will save lives and money and strengthen France's position in the long run even more than a successful war." General Leclerc thought it over and announced, "I am a soldier and I come out to fight, and fight I will."[12] President Roosevelt felt that re-establishing colonial empires was unwarranted and outdated. American intelligence had reported that the Viet Minh were more nationalists than a communist threat to the United States. It is too bad that Leclerc had not taken Mountbatten's advice.

Will said that the war must be stopped, even if others had to be injured or perhaps even killed. The greater good demanded it. He saw the irony in that it was his own country that was fighting the unjust war and

---

[12] *Mountbatten*, Philip Ziegler, 1985, A. Knopf, Inc., page 333.

murdering people in a far-away land. It was up to the people of their own country to join in North Vietnam's "just war" against their own government to stop the evil. He would have to join the "enemy" in order to save his country from itself. Their leaders had gone astray and must be stopped from using its powerful military forces without moral authority. The war was based upon on the thinnest thread of a new unproven and illogical political theory. The world's only superpower following WWII has formulated a new theory upon which America's anticommunist strategy is based, known as the "domino theory". It requires that we fight every communist nation (especially the small ones) overseas so we didn't have to fight them on Main Street, USA. Our leaders fear that if South Vietnam falls, all of the countries in Southeast Asia will fall like toppled dominos soon followed by nations around the world.

Will further stated that Ho Chi Minh holds the reunification of Vietnam far more important than his allegiance to communism, although he was a committed socialist.

Secondly, the free world's new righteous protector, the United States of America, has decided to pursue a war of attrition with a smaller nation, but will find that Vietnam is willing to sacrifice all its military age males, if necessary, to kill every American sent to Vietnam.[13] To the conventionally educated mind of Secretary of Defense McNamara this is unthinkable. Americans would never accept such losses. Already it has been shown that as American causalities have increased, opposition to the war among United States citizens has also increased.

All the rockets, missiles, bombs, artillery and a infantry force of about 500,000 American troops are not enough to stop a people who would fight to the last man, woman and child to secure their freedom. Will felt that this truth was beyond Johnson and McNamara's ability to conceive. They were probably thinking, "The damn enemy is just not logical. Can't they see that they can't win?" Neither Johnson or McNamara can see that such concepts as independence and freedom are very powerful and those who signed our Declaration were under the same spell as the North Vietnamese are now- willing to put it all on the line.

Fighting an attrition strategy against such powerful motivators is tricky- it has always been. The reality is that the U.S. really does not have unlimited troops to put in the field. Political considerations preclude it- the public

---

[13] Over the years of war over 1 million Vietnamese would be killed (some estimates range as high as 3 million) out of a population of 43 million or so. Will did not know the specific numbers at the time, but his assumption of Ho Chi Minh's acceptance of extremely high casualties was correct.

would never put 12,000,000 men and women in uniform as had been done during WWII. Especially to beat up a small country which most people cannot even find on a map.

Further Will pointed out that the U.S. is not fighting in earnest- there are not enough troops on the ground in the theater to win a war by attrition or any other way. There would have to be enough U.S. forces there to successfully invade North Vietnam, fight the NVA units stationed in Cambodia, Laos and South Vietnam and destroy the local Viet Cong militia units embedded throughout South Vietnam.

In its most basic form attrition means engaging and fighting until all the soldiers on one side are dead or wounded.[14] The side with combat capable troops still standing on the field of battle then has a complete victory. But this is expensive in lives even for the winner.[15]

---

[14]Advancing to take and hold the ground or conquer and control an area is not the immediate goal.   The Battle for Hamburger Hill (Hill 937) is a good example. MG Zais, Commander of the 101st Airborne commented that, "This is not a war of hills. That hill had no military value whatsoever… We found the enemy on Hill 937 and that's where we fought him." The hill was abandoned a few days after the U.S. victory, which suffered severe casualties, although NVA losses were estimated to be even greater.   See Lipsman, Samuel; Doyle, Edward (1984*), Fighting for Time (The Vietnam Experience),* Boston Publishing Company.

[15] Grant knew he had access to far more troops than Lee, but he had picked up the nickname "the butcher" because his battles against Lee, when Lee was dug-in and fortified, were extremely costly in lives for the Union soldiers. Grant changed tactics to try to find and fight Lee in the open whenever it was possible.

So the U.S. idea is to attrite the NVA through artillery, aerial bombing ("bomb them back to the stone age"), high tech equipment and U.S. infantry when necessary. The primary infantry forces are to remain those of the country of South Vietnam. The U.S. had been supplying equipment and American advisors to the ARVN (Army Republic of Vietnam) for many years. The ARVN has some first class units, but are generally viewed as unwilling draftees doing their required service- not very aggressive.

The U.S. is fighting with what it has transported to the area, viewing the engagement as a limited war (and keeping one eye on the USSR and one eye on China). The North Vietnamese are fighting with everything they have and know if they keep killing Americans long enough, they will win even if their losses are heavy, but they will never be attrited out. Will said that he believed that it was everyone's duty in the United States to force its government to remove its forces from Vietnam- to "Stop the War". And they, the people at this table, will be in the lead of that movement!

The students at the table all laughed because Will was so wound-up. They decided not to further debate St. Augustine or Ho Chi Minh. Instead they agreed to visit the nearby SDS (Students for a Democratic Society) office, since they were already in the Haight Ashbury District. The Haight was a district of beautiful old Victorian houses and shops which had fallen into disrepair over the years and currently was filled with students from the nearby San Francisco State College (cheap rents). Since the mid-1960's the area had also filled with Beatniks (moved in from North Beach), hipsters, and hippies. It had its own park running east-west just north of the residences and a much larger park, the Golden Gate Park, abutting it on its west side.

It was approaching the end of the school year and soon the summer of 1967 would bring in tens of thousands of young people to the Haight for a "Summer of Love". For the most part the young people drawn there were there to party and attempt to set an example of how the younger generation would run the world with love and kindness and show the older generation (anyone over 30 years of age) that such a thing was possible. Most were not there in 1967 for political rebellion. They were there to be at a "be-in". Marijuana, LSD, and booze fueled the 24 hour a day dancing and partying. Rock concerts, with dancing and light shows at various venues were cheap and frequent. Local talent like the Grateful Dead and Big Brother and the Holding Company were especially popular, but national names were also performing.

The more unconventional the clothing the better. One's eyes could gather in a glace cowboys (made famous by the Red Dog Saloon in Virginia City- where they also carried real side arms), Edwardian suits which were available in the local second hand stores in Haight (prior to the tourist invasion), the Mod clothing of the Beetles and the other British bands that were very popular at the time, and youngsters who were completely unclothed and fornicating in the parks surrounding the area.

Will and the group entered the old office building and went up the stairs to the second floor where there were a couple of desks and some large folding tables stacked high with posters awaiting distribution. A very thin young man was sitting at one of the desks. He was trying to grow a beard but was not really old enough yet so that the beard was thin and scraggily. "Hello gentlemen. I am glad you stopped by because I was looking for Will." He turned and looked directly at Will and said, "Lets take a walk."

Will knew it was serious because this "walk and talk" routine was only used for very private exchanges of information. No telling who was listening to their conversations in the office. As they walked down Haight street the thin bearded man told Will that Will would be studying in Germany this summer. His teacher would be a Stasi (East German secret police) agent who was currently working with the Red Army Faction in West Germany. The bearded man added, "This Stasi agent is the best bomb maker in Europe. When you return you will be the best bomb maker in North America." Will had never heard of the Red Army Faction or the Stasi, but he remained silent.

After the reunification of Germany many years later in 1990 a lot of East Germans held the view that the Nazi's were bad but the Stasi were psychotic killers who were selected specifically because of that trait- no conscience and no hesitation to kill.

CHAPTER 9 Davy Meets Huey

It was February 1966 and Davy was on his way to Fort Rucker, Alabama. It would be five months of instrument flying (flying by looking at the instruments inside the cockpit only), learning to fly the Huey, and tactical training.

Fort Rucker is located in the Southeast corner of Alabama not far from where Georgia, Florida and Alabama meet. It is mostly forest and farm country. The money crop since 1915 has been peanuts. It used to be cotton before that, but a boll weevil invasion forced the farmers to diversify. By 1919 the City of Enterprise and surrounding area lead the nation in peanut production, so they erected a monument of a boll weevil in the center of town. The people were nice and the weather was great except for the normal southern humidity in the summer. The area where the three states met was called the "wiregrass" area by the local folks, but Davy could never really figure out why.

Although the TACS were still around as platoon leaders, they tended to leave the candidates alone. Once in a while at the 5:30 AM morning formation a TAC would hold inspection and ask the question, "Why did God give you that Huey you are about the take flying?" The correct answer was, of course, "so that I can support the finest soldiers in the world with bullets and beans, Sir." The next question was basically rhetorical, "If there were no soldiers in the field for you to support would you be able to back-up to the pay table each month and draw a paycheck?" Of course, the correct answer was, "Sir, Candidate Davis, no Sir!" "So, Candidate Davis, your only worth to the Army and the United States of America is that you fly 'Above the Best', is that correct? "Sir, Candidate Davis, yes Sir!" "Above the Best" was the motto of the First Aviation Brigade", currently assigned to Vietnam. Point made, he would move down the line and perhaps repeat the drill again. All understood that they were soldiers whose specialized training and skills were only part of the team to accomplish the locating, closing with, and killing the enemy by supporting the ground soldiers. Anybody who wanted to do air-to-air combat was in the wrong service. Nobody ever gave the wrong answers, but they kept asking the questions.

The first task at Ft. Rucker was to receive academic training on how all the instruments needed by a pilot to fly without visual reference to the outside of the cockpit worked and functioned. Then he was put into an ancient flight simulator which had been in use since WWII. A canopy was closed over the student's head so that he had to fly by using the instruments only. This device was the "Link Trainer" but was known as the "Blue Canoe". Davy found that this wasn't as easy as it had first looked either.

Once the Blue Canoe was mastered, training was continued in an actual helicopter, the Bell 47, which the Army designated the TH-13T (Training Helicopter 13 with Turbocharger). It was the small bubble top helicopter used in the TV series "Whirly Birds". Davy had seen it as a youngster. It was a stable platform and it was a Bell so it had the same feel to it as a Huey. Plus, it was a lot cheaper to operate than the turbojet powered UH-1 which sucked up 500 pounds, or nearly 80 gallons, of JP4 jet fuel per hour.

Again, it was the same problem- as soon as Davy was proficient at flying on the instruments, things started to fail – it was no mystery, the instructor would either pull the circuit breaker disabling an instrument or he would simply stick a piece of rubber with a suction cup over the top of the instrument. Depending on what instrument was "broken" it could increase the workload substantially. The instructors would say, "You don't lose an aircraft, just because you lose your attitude indicator". To accomplish a let-down and approach without a full complement of instruments was difficult.

Instrument training completed, the day Davy had been waiting for had finally arrived. Huey transition training. The official name of the UH-1 was the Iroquois, but that name was seldom used. At Fort Rucker they flew the old A and B model Hueys which had one window on each side of the cargo compartment. The A & B models had been replaced with the slightly larger D and H models in Vietnam. The newer helicopters could be identified because there were two windows in each sliding side door. But the old ones and the newer ones all had the same flying traits and feel.

The Huey was a single engine jet powered 2 bladed main rotor system with a single 2 bladed tail rotor. Simple aircraft and easy to maintain. But to Davy just starting the jet and watching the exhaust gas temperature climb with the smell of burned jet fuel in his nose was overwhelming to his senses. The instructor told Davy to bring them up to a hover. He told Davy that the last part to leave the ground would be the left rear skid because the aircraft hung tail low and left skid low at a hover for aerodynamic reasons. After takeoff Davy was allowed to just fly around and get the feel for the aircraft, climbs, descents and turns. For Davy it was the most exciting thing he had ever done. The aircraft flew smooth as silk and was as stable as a jetliner. He mentioned his delight to his instructor and was told, "This aircraft only has one bad habit – it's called 'mast bumping'. It will kill you if you put it into negative "g's". Negative "g's" are outside the flight envelope. There must be positive thrust being made by the rotor at all times so it doesn't flap around on its own and hit the mast- the mast will break. The rule is that you must maintain at least a positive .5 "g's". If you are maneuvering around and see your pencil floating around the cockpit you are breaking the rule- and you will probably pay the price. If the engine fails be sure not to let the nose drop, flare it up a little as you lower the collective pitch until you slow back to the airspeed you want in the autorotation. Also, when the engine fails the aircraft will yaw nose left so you will need to add right pedal as you bottom the pitch and bring the nose up. So quick-check the ball and keep it centered because you can also get into mast bumping by getting way out of trim in a slip."

For two weeks Davy got to ring-out the Huey and loved every minute of it. He loved when the instructor gave the surprise engine failures. Before they would bring the engine back on line, Davy could get close enough to the ground to see if he would have actually made the spot he had selected at altitude.

The last part of the training at Fort Rucker consisted of working in a field environment like they would face in Vietnam. The personnel of the training company moved into old wooden barracks at "TAC-X" and practiced formation flying, combat assaults and night operations.

They were also taught how to escape and evade enemy forces and to live off the land by killing, cleaning and eating whatever was available – in this case Alabama rabbit was the Blue Plate Special.

They were given maps of a specific location in Southern Alabama with an X drawn on it. Then they were loaded on busses and dropped off all over the county. If you could land navigate to the X without being captured by the numerous "enemy" troops you were home free. If you were captured, the enemy could "torture" you (up to a limit- monitored by U. S. Army Medics)- but still a very unpleasant experience.

Davy had noticed that one of the men on the bus was an infantry captain, an airborne ranger, whose right shoulder patch showed he had already served a tour in Vietnam before attending flight school. At each stop the bus dropped off 3 "escapees". Davy made sure that he kept within 3 people of the captain. The next group dropped contained the captain, another candidate and Davy. It turned out to be a good idea on Davy's part. The captain said, "It will be dark in 30 minutes. At night it will be dangerous to travel fast through this forest. Too many ditches and the chances are high of getting a branch in the eye if we run. But right now I don't even think they have deployed their forces yet because we are still too far out." The captain looked at the map again, "I know exactly where we are now, so what we are going to do is run as fast and direct as humanly possible till dark. That will put us in a hide here," pointing just uphill next to the X. "Then we hunker down until it is clear to go in." "Stay up- we are not stopping or slowing down." They took off and didn't stop- that captain was like a leopard running fast and hard kilometer after kilometer. At the hide, Davy even curled up and went to sleep. Just before first light, they crawled slowly into the safe zone. The captain's tactics has worked great. And besides, Davy really didn't want any water poured up his nose or anything electrical connected to his private parts. Davy felt that practicing getting tortured was sort of like practicing bleeding, you already know that if you get cut you will bleed- no need to keep proving it. He also knew that if he was captured by the North Vietnamese Army he would be tortured without mercy and then hung up by his wrists with his arms behind his back, pulling the arms out of their sockets. U.S. Intelligence had already confirmed severe torture and solitary isolation of American prisoners. Physical and mental torture- and an indifference to the outcome of such treatment. Nothing will train or accustom one to such treatment- it is practicing bleeding.

On 15 July, 1967 Davy graduated from flight school and was awarded the Rank of Warrant Officer- 1 and pined the Army wings on his uniform. In his pocket, he had orders to Vietnam. With travel time and some leave he would have about 30 days to spend at home with his mother and grandparents before he had to be in Vietnam. Alice was going to fly to LA and meet him there. They had been exchanging letters since they first met at Fort Wolters.

CHAPTER 10 Will Meets Max

Will had just cleared customs at the Frankfurt
Airport. He been instructed to look for a man in a gray
suit and open collar standing near the ground transit exit
doors. There were several who fit that description- suits
of all colors in the 1960's. Great spy thought Will, he can't

even pick something to wear that is unusual. Standing dumbfounded and looking confused, Will was approached by tall man who nodded his head and said, "I have your Taxi waiting outside." The man was wearing shorts and a "T" shirt with a picture of Mic Jagger on the front. Will had no idea what to do, so he followed the man out the door and into a yellow Mercedes taxicab. They drove for several miles into downtown Frankfurt and the man spoke in German to the driver who pulled over and was paid by the Mic Jagger fan. They exited and walked for a block where the man opened a Volkswagen and gestured for Will to get in.

As they drove, Will said, "Who the fuck are you and where is your gray suit?" The man replied in almost perfect English, "You may call me Max and as for the suit, I knew I would see you standing at the exit looking stupid so there was no need for me to give an accurate description of myself and incur any extra risk if we were being monitored or had been infiltrated. Get used to it – there will be a lot of security actions and moves that you will not understand but are for the best. Take my word for it, Sergeant Schultz of Hogan's Hero's fame does not run the West German intelligence services. They are smart and dedicated and they take their job very seriously."

They drove to a small farm near Hanau. Max parked the VW and motioned for Will to follow him into the house. Max made coffee and served them both coffee and cookies at the kitchen table.

"My job is to teach you how to make a simple bomb, which an easy thing to do. I am also supposed to show you how to make it explode at the right time – when you want it to go off. That is a harder job because you must know from reading the newspapers that would-be bombers blow themselves up all the time. I read the International Herald Tribune a short while ago, and I believe the reason you are here is because your group- the "Weather Underground" recently blew up a townhouse in Greenwich Village and lost three of their members in the process. It could have been worse. The paper said that they found 57 sticks of dynamite in the house they were in that did not explode. Children should not play with matches."

I was also instructed to train you primarily to use dynamite because it is readily available in the United States, where it is widely used in mining and construction. Here, I prefer to use plastic explosives for most things, but of course, I have access to whatever suits the job best.

Max took a sip of his coffee and asked, "By the way, do you have any background in electronics?"

"None at all," replied Will. Max frowned, "Well then, let's go to the workshop."

Will noticed what appeared to be a small barn behind the house as they went out the back door. He could see a pile of hay next to the barn and several cows in stalls as they entered the large doors. Wooden stairs led up to an office on the upper floor, but an office without windows. Inside, Will saw an immaculately clean workshop with a long work bench. Above the bench were dozens of tools all placed on trays and hooks.

On the bench Will noticed a dozen small bulbs that looked like flashlight bulbs, except that there was no cap on the end, just wires protruding from the bottom. "These are your sticks of dynamite. That way when you set them off by mistake, my cows will not be bothered." Max also had large sheets of paper and several 6 volt batteries next to the bulbs on the bench. He began by drawing an open and closed circuit on a sheet of paper and explaining basic concepts such volts, amps and ohms.

Will had a pen and was looking around for something to take notes on. Max saw this and said that Will must not write anything down- absolutely no notes. Max said that anything he might write down or sketch during their instruction periods would be burned in the leaf can on the way into the house. They worked through the afternoon and finally Max said, "Enough for today, tomorrow you learn how to solder like a professional- the joint should be shinny and strong. Easy once you learn how to do it. Deadly if you can't do it correctly and a wire comes loose."

Max cooked Wienerschnitzel which Will thought meant breaded veal but Max used thin breaded pork chops and it was very good. Besides, he was hungry.

After dinner Max offered Will a glass of Brandy. Will did not drink and refused the offer. Max smiled and sat the unused glass back on the shelf. "I do not use alcohol either," he said, "I just wanted to see if you did- because you will stay alive a lot longer if you do not drink and your hands do not shake."

Will said, "Where did you learn about bombs?"

"In the Wehrmacht for training and on the Russian front for experience. Actually, I was trained to disarm explosives and not build them. But once you know how they come apart and go together, you can go either direction. You have to be more careful disarming than arming because the enemy military will periodically change some small detail during production that will give you the opposite reaction from what you have been successfully doing to disarm it and blow up a whole city block. We learned that after the war trying to disarm British and American dud bombs".

"Homemade bombs are also difficult to disarm because they are often 'one-off' designs. It can be tricky. But after seeing even one bomb of a particular bomb maker a good explosive expert can tell if a second bomb was designed and made by the same person (or even if some of the surviving parts came from the same manufacturer). The very best bomb makers avoid a signature, but many others just want to get the job done and will do it the way they know works and have used before. They don't care about leaving a signature because they are on a mission from God or a mission to save humanity and are willing eventually to get caught and be a martyr. That's another reason to use a variety of explosives rather than just dynamite. The police will eventually find where the dynamite was stolen and get the batch number. Some dynamite now has a specific marker per batch, which makes identification even easier. Even fingerprints can be a problem on residual debris if the piece was not in an area of high temperature during the explosion. But all that is up to you. At least for now, we will make sure you are safe to use dynamite so that you can make life unsafe for others at your discretion."

Will said, "You don't seem to have any political outlook at all, yet you work for the East German Stasi- the feared secret police of a communist state. Why do you do this?"

"I am too old to worry about the future of mankind or the type of government the people 'deserve' or that God has designed as "natural". I lost my ability to care about human life on the Russian front where millions died all around me. I lost my ability to feel sorrow over the loss of a friend when I had no friends left alive. What else could I do when the Russians found out I was trained in explosives? Should I have stayed in their Prisoner of War camp and died with the other thousands who disappeared? I like my small farm and I have a decent life. I am just asked to make a bomb once in a while. It is the price I pay. But I know the price is steep, because in a few years I will pay the remaining balance in hell, forever. In the meantime, I will leave it to young people like you who are certain they can save the world through killing people by blowing up their cars, homes, subways and banks. And then in a few years I will see you again when you join me in hell. Except you and the other stupid young ones will wonder how you got there- 'we only killed evil capitalists and were on a quest to make life better for all humanity- this must be some sort of mistake'. You are all so spoiled and self-centered that you will still not understand that you are evil- worse than evil- because you kill defenseless innocent civilians. You kill on the cheap- you think that placing a bomb takes courage and you get it planted and then you run away. That is not courage, that is cowardice- for there to be courage there must be risk. Killing with a clock timer is not risk. Killing another person face-to-face, a person who can fight back and possibly kill you first- that is courage. A young German and a young Russian, both out of ammunition and fighting to the death with bayonets and rifle butts and then with fists and thumbs into the eyes and hands around the throat – until the body goes limp and the eyes are glassy and unseeing. That is courage – one man lives and the other dies- but courage on both of their behalves put them together for the final contest. Courage got them both across the battlefield to engage in a battle to the death.

You young ones know nothing of such things. Your heads are filled with useless political theory of various strips which you think is worth killing over. You know nothing of human nature, but you want to rule the people in order to 'save humanity'. You would do better to save yourself in the eyes of God and let humanity take care of itself. It is too late for me, but not for you."

Max continued, "I was never a member of the Nazi party or the Communist party, but I have lived under both and I can tell you there is no difference between the two. The common people live in fear of the government and obey its commands. Any government like the communists which bestows an apartment on you (they have all the keys and are the landlord for all) and provides you with food is also able to withhold the same and kill you slowly – or at least kill your will to resist them. It is good the Nazi's are gone because they also held the power of life and death over the people. The Gestapo was above the law. If you were a Jew, a communist, a gypsy, mentally handicapped, a political protester or even someone reported to them as making an antigovernment statement they didn't even pretend to be the landlord, they simply used the butt end of a Mauser to enter and kill you. Later they would call a locksmith to repair the damage and make new keys for them. Perhaps the former tenants were already dead or in a cattle railcar heading East."

"We need now only to await the funeral of the Nazi's opposite on paper, but brother in practice- the communists. Instead, you and I are here to help the communists kill people and I understand that and accept the consequences. But you actually believe you are here to support 'a peoples' revolution of freedom. You will be a murderer for the Weather Underground as I have been a murderer for the Red Army Faction, which people call 'the Baader-Meinhof Gang'. They are supported by the Stasi and have killed at least 34 people here in West

Germany alone. They really are just a 'gang' of spoiled children who starve themselves when captured in order to get coverage on the evening news. In reality, they could simply hold their breath until their faces turn blue and get the same number of minutes on the television news."

Will had completed his fourth week of training and had not blown-up a lightbulb yet- they had all lit off only when triggered by the correct voltage on the devices he had constructed. He knew the six standard explosive designs and various triggers, including manual activation by wire, clock timing, atmospheric pressure switches (for downing airplanes), weight pressure from above, and radio signal activation. He also knew that it would be easy to make a fatal mistake. Max had to reprimand him several times: once for allowing a wire to slip from the round part of a hold down clip to a point underneath the part of the clip that was screwed down. Max pointed out that if the wire was squeezed underneath the clip the insulation could be compromised and a fatal short occur. Finally, Max was satisfied and gave him a passing grade.

Will felt he now understood how to make rudimentary bombs, he still did not understand Max. He chalked it up to the fact that Max was over 30 years-old (he was 55) and could not be expected to grasp the full meaning of the New Left world order where love was the most valuable law and there would not be a "Stalin" in charge. Max was a man from the period after WWI in Germany where the depression and poverty started early and the pain of an empty stomach as a child was the norm. And growing into manhood on the Russian front where life was cruel, brutish and short was also normal. He was simply trying to live out his remaining years as quietly as possible. He knew life was hard and was trying to survive with as little killing and damage as possible. He also knew he was going to hell- God knew the things he had done to survive.

Will knew it was almost time to leave West Germany and return to the United States. He had learned what he had come for- to make bombs. It did not occur to him that he had heard, without comprehending, what he had really needed to know about making bombs: they tear human beings into bone fragments and pieces of muscle and sinew splattered on walls, streets and cars, *but that it was not too late for him to refuse to join in the slaughter and for him to save his soul.*

Max dropped Will in the crowded area of downtown Frankfurt. Will had been provided with receipts in his name for different youth hostels in various European cities. He was like any other student returning to the U.S. after a summer tour of Europe. He really wished he had seen some of the places on the receipts, like Paris and Brussels. And he was especially drawn to Rome.

Will was waiting on a bench for the streetcar and noticed the young man next to him was reading a copy of the Stars & Stripes newspaper. Will asked, "Are you an American?" The young man said, "Sure, I guess you are too."

Will said he was and was an American college student touring Europe over the summer. The young man said he was an American soldier working at Fifth Corps Headquarters at the old I.G. Farben building. In 1925 Bayer formed the world's largest chemical and pharmaceutical company and built the large building. After the War, since it was still standing, the U.S. Army took it over and still occupied it. He said, "I guess Bayer built another building somewhere else."[16]

Will noticed that the young man had a healing scar on the bridge of his nose with four or five stitches. "What happened?", Will asked.

The young man replied that he had been in a local bar that caters to American GI's when a fight broke out in the far back of the room. It didn't concern him because

---

[16] A few years later the Baader-Meinhof Gang bombed the building destroying the dining area killing Ltc. Paul Bloomquist and wounding 13 others.

he was sitting at the bar near the front door. In a few minutes the "DowDi's" arrived. The GI's referred to the German Police as DowDi's because that was how the sirens on their police cars sounded.

"When they came in, one of them came up to me and told me to 'rouse' and pointed to the door with his nightstick. I didn't know the cop spoke English but as soon as I called him a motherfucker he hit me with his stick."

Will made a mental note to be even more careful and polite at the airport. Certainly didn't sound like the Frankfurt Police were a bunch of Sergeant Schultz's either.

CHAPTER 11 Davy Departs

Davy still had another week at home when Will arrived back at the Torrance house in the first week of August. Their mother was so happy to see them together that she grabbed them both hugged them while she cried for ten minutes. Both their grandfather and grandmother were healthy and happy to see them.

Davy then had a chance to introduce Alice who would be returning to Houston in a few days. During her stay, Alice had fallen in love with the California coast and its beaches from Palos Verdes to Malibu. She had graduated from Denton with her RN degree and was now working in the emergency room of a large hospital in Houston and she would return to her job. Her visit with Davy was fine, but she was disappointed that he had not asked her to become engaged. Davy declared his love for her but wanted to wait until he made it through Vietnam before asking her to marry.

They all ate like kings every evening with meals prepared by Mrs. Davis and her mother and in the evenings had coffee and talked and watched the evening news. Walter Cronkite could not be missed.

Then the day came when Davy had to take Alice to the airport. Alice made him promise to write her a letter each week which she would promptly answer. He said that as soon as he knew his date for R&R he would forward it to her so she could get airline tickets to Hawaii as soon as possible and reserve a hotel room. He had walked her to the plane gate and the final call was announced. As they hugged and gave a last kiss, they both knew that this scene had been played by millions of soldiers and their loved ones over the history of the United States. But that didn't make it any easier.

When Davy returned from LAX it was still before noon. Will said to Davy, "let's go surfing". Davy smiled from ear-to-ear and said, "you bet". So, they got their boards and put them in the back of Davy's VW bus and took off for Torrance beach. They parked and got out and stood on the cliff overlooking the surf to see the waves. "Not breaking very big here, maybe we should go down the coast," said Davy.

"Davy, let's talk first," said Will as he sat down on the parking lot curb, "I don't want you to go to Vietnam. You are my brother and I don't want to see you hurt or killed. They are shipping home 500 dead GI's a week now and its bound to go up if we keep pouring troops in there. And for every dead soldier there are about three that are wounded."

"But that is not the only reason that I don't want you to go. I believe that this war is morally wrong and anyone who supports it is evil. I don't want you to have that scar on your soul. It is still not too late. I belong to a group of people who are actively opposing the war. They have many cells across the United States – some of which are underground and out of the sight of the government. Some of these groups are in touch with underground avenues to Canada where you can cross and live in peace without having to kill for a government which napalms schools and hospitals. Just say the word and I'll have you on your way tomorrow."

Davy's jaw dropped as he stood and looked down at Will, "Have you lost your fucking mind Will? What have they done to up at Berkeley? Have you forgotten about John and how he gave his life for this country? What about Dad answering the call to fight when we both know he was the most kind and gentle man on earth? Don't ever hand me that peace-creep bullshit again. We don't make the decision to go to war – that's done way over our pay grade – its why we elect people we trust to decide if we as a nation must fight and bleed. Only a chicken shit coward would hide in Canada and desert his country when called to fight."

Will stood and looked Davy in the face, "I love you – you are my brother and I want you to live – if I thought I could get away with it I would tie you up and lock you in a car trunk and take you to Canada. But I can see that would be of no use as you would just come back. But what you do not understand is that this whole war is a series of cover-ups to hide the last series of cover-ups. This is not Dad's war where we were the good guys. Here, the people you 'trust' so much have simply bumbled us into a bloodletting contest with a bunch of people on the other side of the world who couldn't threaten us here at home in the U.S. even if they wanted to. It is now simply a conflict so the U.S. can show the world that some third world nation can't kick our ass, like the Finns did to the Russians at the start of WWII. It's now just a publicity stunt to support our image which is eating up our young men like a wood chipper. These men you trust are just incompetent and can't figure a way to get out – you should not trust them. Please think about it. I will not mention it to you again, but if you change your mind let me know. If you do go, I will pray for you every night." After pausing for a moment Will said, "You know, I think we should have a look further down the coast and see if we can find some waves."

They went back to the VW, opened the doors, got in and Davy reached for the ignition to start the van, but then stopped and while looking straight ahead said, "Oh, by the way, I love you too, brother." He then started the van as if he had not said anything and they headed South on the Pacific Coast Highway.

A few days later the Davis family stood in the departure terminal at LAX surrounding a sharp looking young soldier in a kaki uniform forlorn of medals, but adorned with the shinny new wings of an Army Aviator. His boarding pass was for San Francisco International, but he would have to go through the Oakland Army Terminal to get his final boarding pass to a civilian airplane contracted to transport 153 GI's to Cam Ranh Bay, Vietnam.

Will hung around the family home a few more days and then had a short conservation with his grandfather and explained that he was transferring from Berkeley to Michigan State University to finish his degree in philosophy and get a minor in counseling which was not available at U.C. Berkeley. He wondered if he might stay at his grandparent's house while in school up there at least until they came back to the area, if they decided to do so. The offer was gladly accepted as his grandparents would then not have to pay for lawn and snow removal services. Also, they all knew that the house would eventually belong to Will and Davy anyway. Will left and headed to Michigan planning out how to keep the dynamite safe and temperature controlled in the new Weather Underground Safe House in Lansing.

CHAPTER 12 Davy the Slick Driver

Even after many hours on the plane Davy could not sleep. It was dawn and he could see the coast of Vietnam out the right window. He half expected to have to shoot his way off the airplane and jump into a fighting position upon touchdown. His seatmate in the middle seat must have read his mind. He was returning from R&R (rest and recuperation) in Hawaii after serving seven months in the 101 Airborne Division. "Since you are new in country, you are headed for 3 days of boring lectures (while your combat equipment is issued to you) about why we are fighting here to save Truth, Justice and the American Way and to be sure that you use that piece of wood they put in the "C" rations to rub your gums and teeth if you can't brush them and finally a 3 hour lecture on venereal diseases. They will tell you that 50% of the whores in Vietnam have TB and 50% of the whores in Vietnam have VD. "So, I figure that means if they cough, fuck'em."

When the doors were opened on arrival, the first thing Davy sensed was that everything smelled like shit even before they got off the aircraft. The method for disposing of human waste in Vietnam was by burning. So it was hot and stinky. But no enemy charging with fixed bayonets. Cam Ranh was right on the beach in the sand with buildings just like those at Fort Polk. The Army must not have changed the design of their temporary building since 1940. He was assigned a bunk and told he would be called to the S-1 (personnel office) as soon as he was assigned. He read books and jumped bunks as people moved out so as the be closer to the big fan at the end of the building. And went to supply issue and classes.

The Army used the "replacement" system which had not changed since WWII. A unit was deployed to the front and left there. If there was a casualty or someone's time expired (12 months) a replacement would be sent to the unit to keep it filled to fighting capacity. So Davy was in a "repo depo" awaiting his assignment to where he was needed most. Several days later he was called to a building with a number of clerks and maps covering the walls. They told him where he was going and showed him on the map the unit's location. The assignee was also given "orders" of assignment so that he could get on aircraft that would get him closer to the spot where he needed to be. These orders were rarely checked. If you needed a lift all the services would let you on their aircraft if you were an American and in one of the military services or other government agency or a reporter or contractor. All were welcome if there was space.

Davy had been assigned to the highlands at the city of Kontum, an isolated location about 30 miles North of Pleiku. It was near where Laos and Cambodia joined the western border of Vietnam, and was known as the "Tri-border" area.

On the west side of town was a compound of U.S. Special Forces and indigenous forces which were running top secret Long Range Recon Patrols (LRRP) patrols in Vietnam, Laos and Cambodia.[17] Each team consisted of 2 or 3 U.S. leaders and 4 or 5 indigenous Montagnard team members. Like battleships, each team was named for a state in the United States.   Their main mission was to monitor the Ho Chi Minh Trail so the Americans would have some sort of idea of the tonnage being brought south to fight the U.S. and S. Vietnamese armies. This was very dangerous business as there were no friendly troops where the recon teams operated and they operated in the middle of thousands of North Vietnamese Army soldiers.

---

[17] See the book, *Secret Commandos* by John L. Plaster, Simon & Schuster 2004. Their missions were so secret that full reports of their operations were not available for many years following the close of the Vietnam war. Their official name was "Studies and Observations Group" which sounds like a bunch of horticulturists at a convention in Omaha, but they were known by those few who even knew of their existence as "Special Operations Group" or simply as "SOG".

Looking West at Kontum Heliport. 170th AHC living quarters on the right (north) of the heliport.

On the East side of the city of Kontum was another Special Forces compound which was the "B" team for a number of "A" camps which were each located about every 50 miles along the West border of Vietnam. The "A" camps were mainly located at points in Vietnam were the enemy had infiltration routes from the Ho Chi Minh trail into Vietnam itself. The "B" team served as the headquarters and supply depot for the "A" camps in its area.

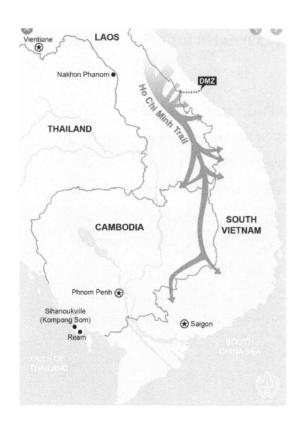

Abutting the "B" team compound on the South was the 170th Assault Helicopter Company. It consisted of about 150 soldiers and support personnel. The compound had a living area and a heliport with enough parking spots for about 30 aircraft. Each parking spot was situated inside an "L" shaped revetment so that mortar and rocket shrapnel damage would be limited. Kontum was nicknamed "Rocket City" and most of the fixed wing airplanes which used the runway located just outside of the 170th perimeter defenses would not shut down their aircraft while loading or unloading. It was a rare day that incoming enemy fire did not rain down for at least part of the day.

The 170th was divided into three platoons: Two troop carrying (lift) platoons of 10 transport aircraft each and a gunship platoon of about 8 UH-1C model armed helicopters. The gunships were of the old style and had been replaced in most units by the newer AH-G Cobra. So the 170th gunships, known as the "Buccaneers", worked mostly inside Vietnam while another unit consisting entirely of Cobras, the 361 Aerial Escort Company, callsign "Panthers" out of Pleiku supported all the SOG missions "across the fence" (border).

AH-1G Cobra gunship. The fuselage was only 36 inches wide.

Each day eight of the 170th troop carrier Hueys were assigned to top secret special operations (SOG) mission. These aircraft were known as "slicks" because of their smooth sides as compared to the gunships which carried an array of miniguns, rockets, 20 mm gatling guns and 40 mm grenade launchers in different combinations. However, even the "slick" had an M60 30 Cal. machine gun mounted on each side for self-defense so it wasn't absolutely slick, but the name stuck.

One pilot would be identified by another as either a "slick driver", "a gunny" or "gun bunny" (if you knew him well enough) or "snake driver" if he flew Cobras.

The first platoon of slicks was known as the "blue" platoon, while the second platoon was the "red" platoon.

Davy had caught a ride on the 170th daily currier aircraft from Pleiku to Kontum. Upon arrival he reported to the Commanding Officer Major George Crawford. Major Crawford had been a pilot for quite a while and had spent his previous tour with the First of the Ninth Cavalry (1/9 Cav) of the First Cavalry Division and was highly regarded by his officers and men. Further, he led them on missions which was not required of him, but admired by the men.

Davy was further assigned to the first lift (the Blue) platoon and reported to the Platoon Leader, Captain Michael O'Donnell. O'Donnell told Davy that he would first take a check ride with the unit instructor to brush-up on his emergency procedures and then start flying missions in the regular rotation with the other copilots (PI). At first he would be assigned only to fly resupply missions to the "A" teams in the area, then he would be assigned to any combat air assaults that were within the boundaries of Vietnam. Only after getting some experience would he be allowed to fly copilot on the SOG missions as those missions were too complicated to allow much training or instruction on the basics. You had to already know how to be a good copilot before working across the fence.

During their conversation Davy had ended every sentence with the word "sir" as he had done when talking with an officer for the past 9 months. O'Donnell said with a smile, "And would you please stop calling me sir after we finish each sentence? A sir every once in a while is fine- or if no higher officers are around just call me Mike" Davy immediately replied without thinking, "Yes sir, I will stop calling you sir." O'Donnell started to laugh with a wide grin and said, "OK, I am going to give you a direct order: You are to address me only as 'Captain Mike' anytime we are in conversation together. You are never to use the word 'sir' to address me unless and until I rescind this order. Do you understand?" Davy hesitated and said, "Yes Captain Mike, I understand." "Good" said O'Donnell.

Davy would have liked to get to know Captain O'Donnell better because he was good natured, quick witted and funny. Sometimes the 52nd Aviation Battalion in Pleiku would assemble all the aircraft which were not committed to a specific mission for the day from each of its four companies to conduct an air assault for the 4th Infantry Division or the ARVN (Army of Vietnam). These aircraft, sometimes up to 20 in number, would meet at the pick-up zone (PZ) and in conjunction with the ground commander make an air mission plan on the spot. Davy watched as Captain O'Donnell briefed the aircrews on the side of the PZ and gave the enemy situation, artillery support, loads per aircraft and how many turn-arounds would be required, etc. He was using a stick to draw the plan on the red clay dirt as he talked. When he finished he fell silent and serious for a moment as he moved his twig around to his front like a swagger stick and said, "Oh, one last thing that you men have got to remember. There are a lot of folks back home depending on what we do out there today. Let's not let them down." Everyone stood there stunned for a moment because they knew that nobody at home had any idea what they were doing there and some of them were likely burning their draft cards at this very moment. After letting it sink in for a few seconds Captain O'Donnell broke out into a wide grin and said, "OK, that's bullshit – we all know that nobody back home gives a shit about what we are doing here today but we are still going to do the most professional air assault Vietnam has ever seen because that's what we do. Are there any final questions?" The crews all had a good laugh and started moving toward their aircraft.

However, within a month Captain O'Donnell and his crew, as well as a recon team he was attempting to rescue, were blown out of the sky with a rocket propelled grenade on climbout. There was no chance that any could have survived because there were two explosions, one when the rocket hit and another probably when the fuel cell exploded. Never-the-less one of the Panther escort Cobras made a pass over the crash site in the canyon at over 200 knots airspeed and was riddled with bullet holes from just that few seconds of exposure. It was not until 1997 that the bodies of the crew and recon team were recovered from a deep ravine in the "Dragon's Tail" area of Northern Cambodia.[18] SOG was a dangerous mission.

Davy was looking for a bunk in the first platoon (Blue platoon) building. The crewmembers had divided the building into small rooms by using the wood from the boxes that the gunship rockets came packed in – so the inside looked like a mouse maze. The walls only went up half way and screen was used up to the corrugated tin roof. The good thing was that there was a thick blast wall all around the building up to the point where the screen started. Davy walked around the building and saw blast damage and shrapnel penetrations to most parts of the wall.

Davy took his refresher "in-county" check ride and did well. He had previously talked to one of his classmates he had seen in Pleiku and his ride didn't go so well. He said the instructor pilot (IP) was an asshole who was on his second tour in Nam and treated him as if he was still a flight student. But his friend wanted to pass the

---

[18] See, *In That Time*, Daniel H. Weiss, 2019 Hachette Book Group, New York.

ride and get flying so he just kept his mouth shut. The IP said that he would demonstrate a simulated engine failure with a touchdown on a flat sandbar in a nearby river. So the IP rolled the engine back to idle and autorotated to the sand bar. Except that just before touchdown the IP let the nose drop so that the skids dug into the sand and stood the helicopter on its nose and then it rolled over on its left side. They both climbed out unhurt and were waiting for assistance after calling in on the survival radio, but Davy's friend could see that the IP was quite shaken by the event and knew his IP orders would be pulled. Davy's friend then asked the IP, "Say there sport, just how many more of those do I gotta do before I'm checked-out?" The IP never responded to the question.

For the next several months Davy flew every day, usually with a different Pilot-in-Command (PC) in order to pick up as much experience and information as possible.

On one flight while cruising at altitude the veteran Pilot-in-Command said, "You know, now is a good time to brief you on my 'catastrophic total-helicopter-destruction emergency procedure.'"

Davy had no idea what he was talking about. "Now you have to understand." The PC continued, loosening his restraints and scrunching into the armor-coated seat, "that this procedure is only to be used when we know for sure that we're tits-up. I mean, if we take a missile up the tailpipe or lose the Jesus nut and have a complete head separation. By the way, Davy, you know how the Jesus nut[19] got its name, don't you? Because when it come off and you watch the rotor blades fly away, all you can say is 'Jesus Christ!' Well, I'm gonna do more than that. I'm gonna stand up and drop my drawers and straddle the stick. And when we hit, its gonna ram that stick home. Then when the accident investigation team inserts on us, they're gonna say 'No wonder the stupid fucker crashed, he had the cyclic stick up his ass.' I want them to try and figure that one out."

Davy must have looked a little skeptical because the PC continued, "No, really, I'm gonna do it. Ain't that right, Bob?"

Bob the crew chief keyed the intercom. "Yessir, if he says he's going to do it, you can bet on it."

"See?" The PC straightened in his seat, stared down at the jungle and said, "I have the controls".

Davy said, "You have the controls."

"I'll show you one right over here that augered in during 'Tet.'" He took the Huey controls and entered a tight right turn near Tan Can where the road turns west to Ben Het.

---

[19] The name refers to the "main mast retaining nut" – a very large nut that holds the rotor blades to the mast.

Then he told Davy to look beneath them at the blackened circle next to the highway.

"Do you know what the fully-armed busting radius of a Charlie model Huey gunship is?" He answered his own question, "right about 100 meters."

Davy did not take his eyes off the blackened scrape in Vietnam's scarred red soil. He couldn't help but think of John.

The PC said, "That's nothing to write home about. There's over 3,000 helicopter holes gracing this lovely countryside. There's a big push on to break 10,000 before we go home."

On a later flight with a different Pilot-in-Command Davy is flying the Huey to the landing zone (LZ) on a combat assault. The PC is leaning back in his seat, his left leg up over the instrument panel.

Davy is thinking, "If I get to be a crusty old geezer someday, I want to remember this moment. We're 10 minutes out of Bad Guy Valley and I'm contemplating death. Maybe Black Bart was right "

Davy had ended up having to take the only available room – Black Bart's. Bart had tried two days earlier to extract a LRRP team in contact and caught a heavy caliber round in the head. Black Bart's room was, in fact, black inside. But it was the writing on the wall that really bothered Davy. On the wall across from the bed, in block letters, was written EVERYBODY DIES – ON A UNIVERSAL SCALE THE TIME IS ONLY A MINOR VARIABLE.

The letters looked white during the day but glowed green at night. When he couldn't sleep and stared at the letters, they seemed to grow to billboard size.

He was used to the room now, and after three months was even beginning to think maybe Black Bart was right. Ten minutes or 10 years; it's all the same. He was 10 minutes out of a landing zone (LZ) with intelligence of heavy AA potential. He had seen many people hurt and dying by now and the world still turned around.

Davy scanned the instruments, then looked out toward the horizon. At 5,000 feet he was bathed in crystalline blue. The air was fresh, cool and clean. The ground, through the inversion haze layer, was a soft green carpet. He watched a sleek Cobra gunship close in with the troop-carrying Hueys. He looked over his left shoulder to check the onboard troops. Regular Vietnamese infantry who were not normally very aggressive.

The hand from outside got him when he turned back forward. It grabbed his jaw and throat like a vise so he could not turn further to the right than center. But in his peripheral vision, he could see an arm extending inside the pilot's siding window on the door. It came in from what should have been empty space at a mile up. Davy jerked up against his straps. Then, just as suddenly as it got him, it released its hold. Still cringing, Davy turned quickly right.

The broad smiling face of the gunner, Gary, filled the side window. He had traveled precariously on the right skid outside the aircraft to the nose. He was still hooked into the intercom system by a long cord and hand-held mike key, "Betcha I scared you, Ha Ha."

Davy's emotions jumped from fear to anger, "Damn, Gary what the hell do you think you're doing? We've five minutes out of an LZ that's supposed to be on top of a whole fucking NVA headquarters and you're up here scaring the shit out of me! Get your ass back behind your goddamn machine gun and stay there!"

The gunner stopped smiling, arched an eyebrow, shrugged his shoulders and started to move aft. As he did, he lost the grip of his left hand. His right held only the mike key. The slipstream caught him, he lost his balance and started to fall. Davy quickly reached through the window but was stopped by his safety straps and only just touched the front of Gary's flight suit. Gary looked into his eyes as he fell away. He was gone.

"Oh Shit! Oh shit! Oh no!" Davy said without keying the intercom. He pounded his knee in frustration, trying to decide what to do. But he knew there was nothing he could do.

"Chalk Two, this is Chalk Four, over."

"Go ahead," said the Pilot-in-Command.

"OK, this is Four. Did you know that your gunner is hanging outside on a monkey strap?"

"Yes, we know- our gunner is just trying to break-in Mister Davis, our PI, in the correct fashion".

Davy turned over the controls to the PC, popped his belts, rolled in his seat and stuck his head out the side window. There was Gary, tethered by a cargo strap and harness, swinging back up to the skid so he could climb aboard.

He still had a mike key in his hand, "Betcha I scared you, ha ha."

Davy's grief turned instantly to disbelief, relief and then rage. He started his tirade without first turning his switch back to intercom- he thought initially he would answer Chalk 4, but the PC had answered. He was still on transmit: "All right now Gary, that's just about enough of this shit! It was OK when you cut the bottom out of my hammock and I jumped in and fell on my ass at Dak To, but this shit is too much!" He stopped to catch his breath.

The radio snapped: "This is Big Horn Six," transmitted the overall ground commander, "There is entirely too much bullshit on this frequency. Mission essential transmissions only."

The flight was arriving at the LZ. "Big Horn Six, this is Panther 36. We're at initial point inbound, over."

"Roger that Panther, the arty prep is finished. It's all yours."

The gunship reconned the LZ. "Blue Lead, this is Panther 36, The LZ is an open area in the valley that should fit V's of three. No obstructions, but we do have a grass fire from the arty. Bring in the flight from the north. We have received negative enemy fire at this time, over."

Gary was back at his gun again and Davy took a final look around before taking the controls for the landing. The Vietnamese troops were all looking back at him the way a guy from Butte, Mont., looks at a New York City cab driver when he thinks he is going the long way around.

As they descended through the layers of altitude, the temperature, humidity and smell of Vietnam returned. It reminded Davy of jumping into a sewage ditch.

The flight turned to the direction for the final approach. The Cobras pulled in alongside. Short final – in over the trees – into the smoke and burning grass to shut off the daylight and choke the crew – no enemy activity yet – maybe it's a cold one – at two feet and still on the go, Davy felt the shifting center of gravity as the troops jumped from the skids.

"Panther 36, Blue flight is coming out."

Gary keyed the intercom: "We got one that won't go; he's hanging on the barber pole."

"Kick the bastard off, now," PC shouted.

Gary looked down at the pleading face of the Vietnamese soldier, then put his boot across the soldier's chest and pushed. The man's hands broke free of the pole and he tumbled off backward still clutching at the helicopter. By this time they were 10 feet in the air and climbing.

Up and over the tree line – and then they popped out of the smoke and darkness. Davy sighed with relief – a cold one – no bullets. All that lay ahead now was a climb to altitude and safety.

As they passed 1,000 feet, Gary keyed the intercom and paused before he spoke. "I know why that guy didn't want to get off." He looked at a ragged hole through the helicopter floor. It was smeared with blood where the soldier had been siting. "He was shot in the ass."

Davy concentrated on maintaining formation, "But that LZ was cold."

"No, sir, I ain't kidding 'bout this one. He took a round through the bottom of the helicopter. It wasn't cold for him."

Davy kept the Huey in the formation and the PC slid down, put his left foot over the instrument panel in his relaxing position and said to the crewchief (CE), "when we get down at the PZ you need to pull the floor panels and make sure that the round missed the fuel cells or didn't damage any linkages or anything else."

They leveled out headed back to the PZ for another load. Someone keyed the mike and very slowly and distinctly said: "Give me liberty or give me death."

A booming voice responded, "This is Big Horn Six. OK, smart ass. I just hope one of you has balls enough to tell me who said that!"

Someone else in the flight of 20 helicopters hesitated for a second, then keyed his mike and said, "I don't know for sure, sir, but I think it was Patrick Henry."

Since Davy had memorized every destination he had traveled to in II Corps while flying copilot, neither he or anyone else had use for a map. He had learned the Area of Operations (AO) for the Vietnam side of the fence like the back of his hand. He was cleared for and then assigned to fly copilot on SOG missions. Never needed a map there either but for a different reason. The Air Force Forward Air Controller (FAC), flying an OV-10 Bronco airplane with the call sign Covey over the top of the team in trouble would visually acquire the Army Cobras and Hueys as they crossed the fence after takeoff from Dak To and direct (vector) them to where they needed to be.

USAF OV-10 Bronco as flown by Covey Forward Air Controllers.

Weird things happened in Laos and Cambodia. The Army flights held high at 7,000 feet or above to stay out of range of the 12.7 mm antiaircraft guns. However, sometimes they would get hit with flack which reminded Davy of WWII movies. Sometimes while holding over the trail whole square miles of ground would explode and the dust and debris rise to 10,000 feet. Then if he looked up he would see 3 small specs in the sky tens of thousands of feet above them. Just before the B-52's would drop their bombs they would announce the location on guard in reference to a TACAN station. Except the Army aircraft were not equipped with TACAN. But Davy figured that Covey, the Air Force FAC had TACAN and would keep them out of trouble. However, he still got a little nervous when he heard the call on guard, "This is Ringneck two-zero on guard with a TPQ alert for 20 nautical miles on the 330 radial from Channel 94 [the TACAN station]. Avoid the area for the next 20 minutes." These "Arclights" did tremendous damage, but the NVA simply filled in the holes or dozed a new path for the trail since it was not paved anyway. In a day or so they were back up to full traffic flow.

Now that he was a full copilot, Davy had to show them that he was qualified and had the right stuff to command an aircraft. It was similar to the copilot pathway. If a copilot was promoted to Pilot-in-Command (PC) he could initially expect missions inside Vietnam only, mostly supporting the "B" team and the "A" teams until the 170th Commanding Officer could evaluate his performance as a PC. Then a decision as to assigning the new PC to the SOG mission would be made. Further, if a pilot made PC and felt he should not or could not be assigned to the SOG missions, he could decline and simply fly in Vietnam. All of the crewmembers supporting the SOG LRRP Special Operators were volunteers. There was never any kickback or even a bad word said about someone who wished to pass on the Sneaky Pete mission. The highly trained unconventional fighters who made up the teams would probably prefer those who wanted to be there to those who had been forced to support them in their complicated and dangerous missions.

Davy wanted to become a PC with his own aircraft and crew. And he wanted to fly missions over the fence. He wanted to work with the elite warriors of SOG who routinely faced odds on the ground that would be unthinkable for lesser men. He would get his wish, but not in the manner he imagined.

CHAPTER 13 Will's Personal Assignment

Will had settled in at his grandparents house in Lansing. Most of the neighbors knew him from summertime visits and welcomed him back. The neighbors did not know that there were six cases of dynamite in the basement or Will might have gotten a slightly cooler reception.

He had been instructed by his home Weather Underground cell in Ann Arbor to make sure he registered at Michigan State and carried at least 12 units so that he could continue his "2S" (secondary school) deferment from the draft. Of course, he would never report if drafted, but they needed him in Lansing and not Canada.

Will made sure the grass was cut and the outside of the house was well maintained in order not to draw an attention to himself.

Nothing was done by telephone. All orders for bombs were delivered by visitors who for all appearances looked like regular college friends stopping by for a visit. They came in the afternoon and would leave no later than 10 PM so the neighbors could see Will was not running a party house and was probably just studying with a friend.

In the next two years Will made at least 25 bombs which were used against various targets like the U.S. State Department, the Capital Building, NYPD Headquarters and the Presidio Army Post in San Francisco. The Weather

Underground wanted precise bombs that were designed to terrorize and destroy buildings but not necessarily kill human beings. Most explosions were set off after hours (which still put the cleaning crews at risk) or a bomb threat was phoned in prior to the explosion. All-in-all, it was simply lucky that there were no more killed than their own three amateurs in Greenwich Village.

Then things started to change. The Weathermen went into deep cover and formed a new group called the "May 19th Communist Organization" combining with the Black Liberation Army. The date of May 19th was Ho Chi Minh's birthday. Bomb orders continued but other violence of intended lethality also increased. A Brinks truck at Nyack, NY was held up and one of the Brinks guards was shot and killed. Two police officers were also shot and killed at a roadblock set up to apprehend the killers. And amateurs were getting back into the bombmaking business. William Morales of FLAN blew his hands off and then escaped from custody at Bellevue Hospital in New York City. Susan Roenberg and Tim Blunk were arrested at a rented warehouse in Cherry Hill, New Jersey with 200 sticks of dynamite and 100 blasting caps.

The next order that came to Will was different than all the others. The FBI and the NYPD had set up a "Joint Terrorism Task Force" in the FBI New York City field office to coordinate all federal, state, and local law enforcement and intelligence regarding terrorism. The police were the only active enemy of the revolution in the United States since the military was forbidden to engage in domestic law enforcement.[20] Accordingly, the police were known as "pigs" to the Weather Underground and their revolutionary companions. Will was told that to preserve the revolution these pigs must be stopped from forming such alliances and they must be shown immediately and with the penalty of death.

Will was given the name, home address and a photo of NYPD Captain Timothy Burke who commanded the new task force. Will's contact said, "We want it done at his home in Long Island. It is unlikely that we could get close enough in the city, especially after blowing up NYPD Headquarters once already. And one last thing, this has to be done right so were want you to take care of it

---

[20] Of course, each state has their own militia known as the "National Guard" which the governor can use for emergencies such as natural disasters and to restore order in the event of a riot. In fact, most are not well trained in shoot-don't-shoot decisions while deployed for riot control as evidenced by the shootings at Kent State. However, National Guard units generally do not gather intelligence for criminal purposes. If a National Guard unit is brought on active duty (federalized) under title 10 of the U.S. Code, it then is subject to all the restrictions which apply to regular federal troops. Notwithstanding other restrictions, the federal military does share "signals" (electronic) intelligence from various agencies (NSA, DIA, etc.) with federal civil authorities. A secret operation, code-named "Minaret", was set up by the NSA to monitor the phone communications of Senators Church and Baker, as well as major civil rights leaders, including Martin Luther King and prominent U.S. journalists and athletes who criticized the Vietnam war. However, an internal review by NSA concluded that the program was "disreputable if not outright illegal". See, *The Guardian*, September 26, 2013.

yourself. When you finish the bomb, you drive it to New York and you plant it and you make sure it goes off and kills Captain Burke. We do not want to hand this off to a different cell or to a part-timer."

Will nodded and his contact departed.

He decided on a very powerful but simple bomb with a trip wire ignition. He made the bomb, told his neighbors he had to leave for some university research and asked them to keep an eye on the house and then started for New York.

He drove by Captain Burke's house several times to get a look at it, then parked down the block several afternoons to see what time he usually arrived home. It was in a middle-class neighborhood and was an average size 3 or 4 bedroom house. He did notice that the houses were set back on the lots in relation to what he was used to seeing. He decided that he would set the bomb off to the left side of the driveway in a flower array and run an extremely thin wire across the driveway about a car length from the street. He had painted the trip wire dark gray so it would hardly be noticeable against the driveway. He only needed it to be a half of an inch off the driveway surface to trigger the bomb when the car drove over it.

He wore coveralls with the words, "Joe's Landscaping" stenciled on the back in case someone saw him and was curious. He estimated that he could place the bomb in less than a minute. He then waited until about 30 minutes before he estimated Captain Burke would be home in order to ensure as much as possible that no one else would trip the wire early.

At 5:30 PM he took the square box, a small amount of wire and a large nail and walked to the driveway. It was still light outside but he saw no pedestrians and as far as he knew, no one saw him. He placed the box, shoved in the nail and stretched the wire. Then he flipped a toggle switch on the box and went back to his car across and down the street a short way.

It turns out that Captain Burke was a man of habit. At six o'clock he came down the street, but instead of driving up the driveway he stopped at the mailbox. Will then saw something that terrified him- a little girl about 5 years old ran from the house yelling "Daddy, Daddy's home!" If she ran down the driveway to her father she would be killed.

Will could not let this happen. He jumped from his car and ran past Captain Burke and grabbed the little girl. Seeing something flash past him while he was going through the mail Burke instantly moved toward what he now recognized as a man moving toward his daughter.

He was already reaching for his weapon and yelling, "Stop motherfucker or you're a dead man!

Will had stopped just in front of Captain Burke's daughter to stop her from moving further down the driveway. Burke yelled, "On the ground, face down, on the ground."

Will yelled back, "Tell her to go into the house now! There is a bomb trip wire in front of you on the driveway and if you step on it coming toward me, she will die with us. Get her in the house now!"

Captain Burke seemed stunned for a moment and then told his daughter to go into the house and close the door and dial 911. Burke's daughter turned and ran into the house. Burke then told Will to get on the ground again, face down. Will complied with the order. Captain Burke then said, "How do I get to you without setting off the bomb?

Will replied that the wire was strung across the driveway only and right now it crossed the driveway just in front of the car's front bumper.

Captain Burke slowly walked up the lawn and handcuffed and searched Will. Burke said, "Why did you stop when you could have let me drive over it?"

Will answered, "I would have killed you because I fight a just war and you are the enemy. But the child is an innocent. 'If anyone causes one of these little ones who believe in me to stumble, it would be better for them to have a large millstone hung around their neck and to be drowned in the depths of the sea.' I was worried that harm might come to the child."

Will was arrested and remanded into federal custody for further proceedings.

CHAPTER 14 The Rescue of Team Ohio

When Davy had 5 months "in country" and had planned to be in Hawaii in a month or two, loving on Alice and sucking down umbrella drinks. However, when he had not heard from her for several weeks he got a letter explaining that she was extremely sorry but that she had met the man of her dreams at the hospital in Houston where she worked. He was an MD in the gynecology department and had a great future in medicine in his new practice. She and Davy had great fun together, but she had only one chance to claim her life's partner and would do it while he was still available. She, of course, told Davy what a wonderful man he was and some girl would be very lucky to have him as their life partner and husband. He did not respond, but got drunk on Jack Daniels instead, which could be purchased at the PX in Pleiku for $1.25 per fifth. After drinking most of the Jack he composed a letter to Alice explaining that it was probably the best for all concerned that they did not meet in Hawaii because he was currently suffering from a severe case of the clap and was still undergoing the penicillin shots to cure the problem. However, on the bright side, if she still wanted to meet him and were to get a case of gonorrhea, she could have her new friend fix her up for nothing. He never sent the letter and later in life was glad he did not.

The good news was that Davy performed well as a PC and was cleared to fly over the fence. The staging area for all these missions was Dak To, just a few miles from the border. It was hot, dusty and dry, but as close to the teams in the field as one could get and remain in Vietnam. The only good thing it had to offer was a mountain stream that ran parallel to the runway with water that was cool, clear and clean. Right out of the mountains with no villages above to ad human waste or pig shit to the flow. There were a couple of shacks there, one for the radios and operations tracking and one for the "Brightlight" team which was the code name for the recon team which was on instant reaction duty for the week. The Brightlight team could be off the ground in a matter of minutes if required to combat assault in to assist a team in the field that was being overrun or needed some other kind of help.

Dak To Staging Area. Note commo shack in center of photo.

The helicopters were parked in a single file for almost half the length of the strip. Some of the crewmembers were stripped to their boxer shorts playing touch football on the runway. Others were sleeping on hammocks slung between the brace poles ("barber poles") inside the helicopters, or along the helicopter sides in the shade. Each time a transient helicopter would land and hover up the runway for fuel, the football players would run for cover from the rotor wash and the grit that would sandblast each side of the runway. Most of the sleepers would not be awakened, or would just drowsily try to shield their face, then fall back into a few more fitful minutes of half sleep. But it really didn't matter who tried to run and who didn't, because everyone's body was covered with sweat and fine sand.

A Recon Team waiting for takeoff and insertion.

About midway down the line of helicopters was the radio shack sporting many antennas for different spectrums. The radios crackled with the sounds of traffic and the tone of the secure voice (encrypted transmissions) kicking in. The heat seemed ever more oppressive here because of the thirteen bodies crowded into the ten by twelve-foot shack. Twelve of these men were the PC's and the thirtieth was the Special Forces Captain hunched over the rows of radios. The pilots stood hushed as the Captain scribbled notes from traffic on three nets, then he stood and, without turning, put his finger on the map that covered the entire wall above the radios. "Okay, this one has just been declared a Prairie

Fire emergency. Here is the LZ (Landing Zone) for pickup. The team will rendezvous there in 40 minutes." Team Ohio was in trouble. "They're in contact and on the run at this time. Their present position is 1.5 kilometers from the LZ. Covey will brief you on the updated tactical situation while you are airborne enroute. There is one KIA at last report." The news was not unexpected. The pilots had been monitoring the radios since the first sign of trouble. These were reconnaissance teams in the field and the last thing they needed or wanted was enemy contact. Once they had to start shooting, their mission of intelligence, and their usefulness, was over. Ohio was a team of 10 men, now nine, and no matter how good, they could only last a matter of time deep in enemy territory where they faced companies and battalions of NVA.

Davy wondered what Team Ohio's mission was. Maybe to count truck traffic down the Ho Chi Minh trail. He didn't know- they had no "need to know". They weren't told. Only to put them in and pick them up. He wondered if there would be any left alive to pick up. As the pilots started to move out of the shack, one asked, "Is the KIA US or indigenous?" Team Ohio, like the other teams, consisted of two Americans and the remainder of locally recruited Montagnards. The US Special Forces men were the team lead and the second in command who also served as radio man. The Captain sat down again in front of his radios, and still without turning, answered, "Don't know."

Everyone knew there were no more questions. The pilots filed out and began to jog to their helicopters. The football players immediately took their cue in this scene that had been played many times before and broke into runs for their birds. Rotor blades were already untied and ready for start. Trousers and shirts were pulled on. Davy reached into the cargo area and got out his "chicken plate". He strapped on the 15-pound chest armor which was an inner piece of steel with an outer layer of thick ceramic material. It was supposed to stop up to a 30 Cal. round. The crewchief and gunner both also wore chicken plates and each sat on one for good measure.

Davy was the flight leader today for the first platoon, so his call sign was "Blue Lead". He stood on the skid, looked down the line to check his flight, then climbed into the cockpit. He snapped into the thick nylon straps that went over his shoulders and around his waist, then slid the 38 Special sidearm from his right hip to a position between his legs so that the weapon was directly over his genitals. The seat was armored which gave protection from the sides, bottom and rear, but with the exception of the steel and ceramic chick plate chest armor, the front of his body was exposed. He laid his hands and feet on the controls for start and felt at home again. This is where he had spent most of the last year and a half. This bird was his and it was part of him. It wasn't a conscious thing. He didn't try to make it so, but it was. This helicopter had become an extension of his body like an arm or a leg. And like an arm or a leg, he could feel through it. Its state of health, its load and even the texture of landing surfaces transmitted up through its skids.

The crew chief and gunner on this crew worked together like clockwork. In flight, the crew chief and gunner both had the same role; to man the M-60 machine guns on each side of the Huey and to give obstruction avoidance clearance to the pilot during pickup or drop-off operations. On the ground, the crew chief owned the aircraft. He was responsible for all upkeep and maintenance to the helicopter. The gunner cleaned the weapons and assisted the crew chief. Each day on the first flight the M60's were test fired. The worst sound in the world was a single "pop" from one of the guns. It was also very embarrassing for the gunner whose primary job was to make sure every night that the machine guns were disassembled, repaired and cleaned. A "single shot" machine gun would not keep the bad guys heads down in an LZ.

During the trying times on a mission, the entire crew melted into a single unit. The pilot could only see

180 degrees centered on the nose. For the rear half of the helicopter clearance while hovering down into jungle holes he had to depend on the gunner and crew chief. They had to work as a team and talk the pilot down. A tail rotor or main rotor strike as the ship maneuvered into a jungle hole for pickup might cause the aircraft to crash. The crew chief and gunner had to tell the pilot which way to swing the tail while they were descending, without cutting out each other on the intercom, and coordinate the amount of tail movement available on each side so that the extremely fast-moving tail rotor would not contact any obstruction. Any strike to the tail rotor at its great speed likely would cause loss of directional control and a crash in the LZ. The forty-eight-foot main rotor blade turned at 324 revolutions per minute, pushed by a 1,300 SHP turbojet. By contrast to the fragility of the tail rotor, the main rotor system would take considerable punishment before control was lost. The large blades turned only turned one fifth as fast as the tail rotor and had a strong steel forward spar which could cut into some foliage without being damaged.

The recon teams and the Covey Air Force FAC, flying with an experienced ground soldier known as the "Covey Rider" chose the LZ's. Sometimes the selected LZ would not allow for the descent of the helicopter all the way to the ground. Then rolled-up flexible ladders had to be deployed out each side. These extended 12 feet below the skids on each side.

With most of the area covered with 100 foot trees in triple canopy jungle, there were some areas where a helicopter could not land at all within a distance were the recon team could reach. In such cases, 100 foot ropes (strings) had to be used for extraction. The helicopter would hover above the jungle and the crew would throw weighted bags with coiled rope down through the trees to the team below. A major problem with using strings was that there were only four strings on each aircraft, so multiple aircraft normally had to be used. The primary concern was the hover time above the trees while the strings were dropped and team were hooking up into a swiss seat or stabo rig. Exposure time was critical and a hovering helicopter was a sitting duck. Ideally the exposure time would be measured in seconds. However, for string extractions it jumped to minutes, with more shooters having the time to gather beneath and unload a magazine of AK47 rounds into the helicopter sound above them.

The crew chief was Bob, a 19-year-old farm boy who had been around machinery all his life and treated this bird with the love he would give his best John Deer. The gunner was an 18 years old draftee from San Francisco named Vic, who, when not wearing a helmet, wore a red bandana around his forehead to keep his thick curly hair from falling in his eyes. The copilot for today was Rick, 20 years old from Southern California. The aircraft, the PC, the crew chief and gunner had been together now for four months. Four months in Vietnam was an eternity. Most crews had turned over twice since they had come together due to hostile fire or rotation. The copilot Rick, of course, rotated to fly with different PC's to gain experience before moving to the PC position himself.

Davy could hear the whine of the jet turbine engines and see the blades on the Cobra helicopters in front of the Hueys began to turn. He pulled on his helmet, called clear and engaged the starter trigger. He glanced at the voltmeter as the turbine slowly growled to life; thirteen percent blades turn; 40 per cent trigger release; up to operational RPM; radios on. There were three radios used for commo in the helicopter. VHF for inter-flight communications of the Blue platoon, UHF for coordinating with the cobra (Panther) gunships and the Covey FAC, and FM to talk with the ground teams with their backpack PRC 25's.

The radios were hooked up through a selector box to each crewmember so that the radios could be monitored individually or all together. The pilots usually listened to all the radios at once because the information on each frequency was necessary for coordination and keep abreast of the situation. This took a practiced ear to listen to three transmissions at the same time and to hear all that had been passed. To make matters worse, the hotter things got, the more traffic there was on the radios. In addition to the external transmissions received, the pilot also had to hear the intercom instructions from his crew while maneuvering in tight areas and hover holes. And the crew's voices often had to compete with the roar of their M-60 machine guns when they keyed their intercom. After 7 months of practicing the art, Davy had become an expert at digging out the necessary bits and pieces of information necessary for survival. He was good and he knew it. Since he had been in country he had studied, watched and learned every technique and trick to accomplish the mission and ensure survival. The only fear he felt now was not a fear of dying but fear of making a mistake. To catch a bullet in the head or to be blown to bits by an enemy rocket propelled grenade on final approach to the team was fate. But only if there were no mistakes made.

Over the months, he had seen pilots be too fast on approach to stop at the LZ or lose sight of the LZ and have to make a go-around, only to be riddled by bullets over the same area they had safely traversed moments before; exposure time was critical. They had to do everything twice because of some mistake and therefore had twice the exposure. He had seen other mistakes, like pilots that, in the heat and confusion of battle, had not heard or taken the instructions from their crew and struck a tree with their tail rotor and crashed and burned and died in the LZ. To catch a bullet like that, or to die like that, was not fate. It was a mistake. More than his own safety, he worried about a mistake that might cause the life of one of his crew or the troops on board. But he was good and his crew was good, and because of that, today they were "Blue Lead".

"Lead, three is up," cracked the VHF.

"Roger, three."

"Lead, four is up."

"Roger, four."

"Blue Lead, this is Panther 26," transmitted the Cobra gunship leader on UHF.

"The Panthers are up. Over."

"Roger 26. Stand by one."

Davy let the mike trigger on his stick slip from the transmit position to the first indent intercom position. "Bob, jump out and see what the problem is with two."

"Okay."

Bob unstrapped and started to jump from his bench seat, but stopped halfway out when he saw the blades on the number two Huey begin to turn slowly. He keyed his hand intercom. "They just now are cranking, sir." Now the blades on the first four of the six Hueys in line were turning. Blue Lead and Blue Three would be the pickup birds for Team Ohio. Blue Two and Blue Four would act as "chase" birds for the pickup birds in case one or both of the pickup birds were shot down. Accordingly, Blue Two and Blue Four would stay at altitude and watch the show unless needed.

Two additional Blue flight aircraft were left at Dak To as spares to replace any birds lost during the Team Ohio extraction mission so that the next mission would not be delayed for lack of assets.

Although the Hueys were designed to carry as many as 11 passengers, it would take two aircraft to pick up the remaining nine team members. There were several reasons for this. First, the birds had a rather heavy mission weight with crew, ammo and special jungle extraction gear set up in the cargo area. There were four 100-foot ropes (strings) anchored to the floor and a 12-foot aluminum bar-runged rope ladder for each side rolled-up in the center of the floor. These devices made possible pickups where landing was impossible. The second reason was that turbine engines and airfoils don't perform at their best when it is hot and humid, and here it was hot and humid.

In front of the Huey line facing 45 degrees away from the runway were six cobra gunships which used the call sign "Panther", three of which were running. The attack helicopters normally worked in pairs known as fire teams. Three together were called a heavy fire team. The extra gunship carried a 20-millimeter Vulcan cannon to be used to destroy enemy 51-caliber machine guns at standoff range. The cannon looked like a giant Gatling gun. It looked to run almost one-third the length of the Cobra. The other two gunships were to escort the Hueys into and out of the LZ. The escort Cobras and were armed with 52 17-pound rockets in the wing stores and pods and a 7.62 mini-gun and 40-millimeter grenade launcher and turret. The mini-gun could fire up to 4,000 rounds per minute and looked like a garden hose spraying lead when fired. These Cobras would be used to suppress enemy fire during the extraction. They were much better than any other type aircraft for close support. Not because of massive ordnance, but because of their pinpoint accuracy and instantaneous response. The three gunships that did not crank were on ready standby in case the other heavy fire team expended their ordnance.

"Blue Lead, Blue Two is up."

"Roger two."

"Panther 26, this is Blue Lead. We're ready. You can call us out if you like."

"Roger that, Blue Lead."

Davy watched the Cobras hover out on the runway, and one by one take off to the West. As the last Cobra lifted off, he brought his helicopter to a hover and taxied into position for a takeoff. This flight flew loose trail with almost a quarter-mile separation between aircraft. It wasn't a pretty formation, but it had a purpose. It forced the enemy anti-aircraft gunners to choose a target. And if one bird was hit, the others could survive by taking evasive action. Also, very rarely would the landing zone be large enough for a close formation approach. Triple canopy did not lend itself to large helicopter formation tactics. With his left hand, Davy increased the collective pitch power control and with his right, moved the cyclic stick forward for take-off.

As Davy took off, he temporally flew the helicopter a bit sideways so the wind could blow through his window. The rush of cool air felt good. As he came through the haze at 2,000 feet, he looked to the mountain range that ran between Dak Seang north to Dak Pek. They were green and beautiful mountains, with waterfalls and fresh cold streams. This was one of the few areas left that hadn't been defoliated or carpet bombed. As they passed 4,000 in climb, Ben Het, and beyond it to the

West, looked like the battle area it as, a moonscape of barren hills crated with thousands of tons of ordnance. Many of the craters were in neat rows, signifying that the B-52's had awesomely shown their presence. Davy leveled at 7,000 feet and kept the Cobras in sight. They were about 2 miles to his front. It was cold now and his sweat-soaked flight suit retained little body heat. He looked at the co-pilot and saw him with his hands clasped on his lap and his shoulders raised. He was shuddering. Davy wondered if all the shaking was from the temperature. There would be about 8 more minutes before they reached the LZ area.

"Covey, this is Spad 01 with you at one-four thousand. We are on the 260 for twenty-two off Channel 94. Over."

U.S. Air Force A1E dropping ordinance.

The Air Force close air support aircraft, Spad 01 and Spad 02 were checking in with the Forward Air Controller, Covey. Covey was the orchestrator of this symphony of battle. Davy was relieved to hear the Spad call sign. These were the old A1E World War II type prop aircraft, but this was World War II type combat and these machines did exactly the type of job that they were designed for. He was glad because close air support was a hit or miss proposition. Sometimes A1E's showed up and sometimes F4's. The F-4 was a fine sophisticated war machine, but the F4's were moving so fast that sometimes they couldn't initially spot the LZ. Four hundred knots was just great for bombing North Vietnam, but for dropping close support ordnance Davy liked the A1E. And Davy never could remember a time when an A1E had to leave to get fuel in the middle of an extraction.

"Roger, Covey," the Spad 01 continued. "The mailing list follows. Zero-one has eight Mark 82 high drag and two 500's. Two is wall to wall with CBU 22. We're each packing 1,000 rounds of 20 millimeter and six rounds of 38."

Davy knew Spad 01 and he knew was a good and aggressive pilot. He had never been to Peliku Air Base to meet him or ever even talked to him on the radio, but he knew his work and he knew he knew he did a good job.

Spad 01 continued. This time he was talking to his wing man, Spad 02,

"Okay two, flip 'em up, set 'em up, coming hot. We're gonna kill."

The Forward Air Controller put the Spads to work on the high ground around the LZ. The LZ was located in the valley between two small ridgelines. The team had reached the valley and was ½ kilometer from the LZ.

Enroute, the Cobras had monitored the radios and had seen the Spads put in on the superior terrain.

"Covey, this is Panter 26. We're gonna orbit three miles east at 9,000 until you're ready for us."

Davy saw the Cobras break into a left orbit and continued until his flight was the same distance from the LZ, but about a mile north of the Cobras.

"Covey, Blue Lead. We'll be waiting just north of the Panthers. Over."

"Roger, Blue Lead."

Panther PC WO1 Terry Crump hit with flack while holding over Laos.

Even as Covey was rogering his transmission on UHF, Davy could hear the team Ohio radio man calling Covey on FM. The transmission was weak. He was out of breath from running and there was small arms fire in the background.

"Covey, Covey, this is Romeo Alpha 56. Romeo Alpha 56. Over."

"Romeo Alpha 56. This is Covey. Over."

"Covey, the one-zero is KIA. We are approaching the LZ. Will they be there to pick us up?"

"That's affirm Romeo Alpha 56. We're just waiting on you. Over"

"Okay, out," was his breathless reply.

The team leader, the "one-zero" was dead. That was their second man killed.

Davy was watching a Spad making his run on the west ridgeline when just short of his target the AIE turned at an almost vertical bank and released a hail of bombs about halfway up the east ridgeline. Spad 01 keyed his mike.

"Sorry about not hitting the area I was cleared into Covey, but I needed to take care of that quad 50 that was bothering me from over there."

Davy knew that Spad 01 had just saved his life. That weapon would have brought down his helicopter for sure. He swore that if he ever could get a hop to Peliku AB, he would buy 01 drinks all night and give him a big bear hug.

The team had now reached the LZ, but was still in heavy contact. Covey moved the Spads out and held them over the top.

"Panther 26, this is Covey. We are ready to start. Do you have me in sight?"

"That's affirm, Covey. Panther 26 has you in sight."

The Cobras broke from their orbit and headed towards the LZ. Davy rolled out of his left turn and set a course to arrive over the LZ at the same time.

"Okay, Panther 26. I'll give you a mark on the LZ."

The Covey OV-10 rolled into a wingover and steep dive, flew up the valley at low level and when he was directly over the LZ, he called out "Mark, mark."

Davy saw the area, but could not make out the LZ from his angle. The whole valley looked about the same, tall trees and thick vegetation, but the Cobras were closer, so maybe they had seen it.

"Roger, Covey. We have a good tally on the LZ now. We'll head down and have a look."

The first and second Cobras nosed over into high speed dives. The 20-millimeter ship stayed at altitude.

"Panther 26, this is Covey. The team is being pursued to the north up the valley, so most of the bad guys are to the south of the LZ. You might want to soften that area. Over."

The Cobras were just passing over the LZ low level for their first look. As he passed over the LZ, Panther 26 could feel the thuds in his fuselage of impacting rounds. The front seater opened up on the mini gun.

"Roger that, Covey. The Panthers are receiving heavy fire. We are going to do some close shooting to the south side of the LZ before we bring the Hueys down. Notify the team to stay low."

As he finished speaking, he moved his left thumb from the radio transmit button to fire button and began launching pairs of rockets. The Cobras made six more gun runs. Blue Lead had descended to 4,000 feet directly over the LZ.

"Blue Lead, this is Panther 26. I guess we are ready for you now. The situation down here is really messy. Do you have a good tally on the LZ. Over?"

Davy thought he did, but there were two areas near each other that could possibly be the landing zone.

"Can you give me a new mark on it?"

"Roger."

It was the same one Davy had been looking at.

Panther 26 continued his briefing. "The LZ is a small hover hole. I can't tell if it is a sit down because of the vegetation and grass near the bottom. It may be too small even to get to the bottom. You might have to use the strings or ladders. From the smoke here, the wind is light and variable and should be no factor. The majority of the enemy troops are to the south of the LZ in the valley, but are closing around the LZ at this time. Your approach and departure should be from the north to avoid the heaviest enemy concentrations. It will be a hot escort into the LZ."

Davy knew that it was going to be a hot escort, but the Panthers always announced it anyway. It was disconcerting for rocket explosions to go off underneath the helicopter and think they were meant for you. Instead, they were there to keep the enemy's head down as you passed over. Yet, sometimes the Huey would return from a mission with shrapnel in the tail boom from a "too close" hot escort.

Davy hoped that he could get by without using the strings or ladders. Those were harder pickups, but more important it took longer. Every second at a hover under fire was extremely critical exposure time.

Davy keyed his intercom and asked the crew if they had all received and understood the situation. They all did. He locked his inertial reel shoulder harness, took off his sunglasses and lowered the clear visor on his helmet. He squinted his eyes adjusted to the bright sunlight. The clear visor offered no sun protection, but Davy knew that darkness fell in midday in hover holes, and this was going to be in a hover hole.

"Blue Lead is out of 4,000."

"Okay, Blue Lead. We'll pick you up inbound," replied Panther 26.

The gunships had set up a race track pattern with the inbound parallel to what would be Blue Lead's final approach. They would fly faster than a Huey, but would adjust their breaks, so that one gunship would be inbound behind the Huey at all times.

Davy lowered the nose to pick up red-line airspeed, put the collective pitch to the bottom and entered a series of descending steep turns. He wanted to get on the deck through the effective range of small arms fire with the least possible delay. From 1,500 feet and below to the surface, anybody with a rifle who could see you could shoot you. Flying final on the deck offered protection in that not as many enemy could see you. The vertical speed indicator read 2,200 feet per minute descent. Davy made a forced yawn and rocked his jaw back and forth to clear his ears. As they descended, the heat and humidity filled the cockpit. He added power and leveled out on final just outside the gunship pattern. The first sound that he heard was a rhythmic signature of an AK-47, but he knew that it was nothing to worry about, because the sound was behind him and he wasn't taking any hits. They were shooting at his sound up through the trees. That's why he was low and fast. By the time they could react to his presence, he was gone. The outbound gunship made a steep turn inbound to pick him up.

"Panther 26, has you covered lead."

"Roger."

At this altitude, it was impossible to see the LZ, but Davy had picked out points while still at altitude that he could reference. Davy's chase bird, Blue 2 was still at altitude and gave Davy "vectors" to keep him on track to the LZ, "OK Lead, the LZ is at your 12 O'clock at 150 meters." The airspeed was still near red line. Too damn fast. He brought the nose up and lowered power to dissipate airspeed. His chase bird offered, "LZ still at your 12 O'clock at 100 meters. Suddenly, the area underneath the helicopter exploded with rockets fired by the inbound Panther. Out of the corner of his eye, he saw the co-pilot jump against his straps. He'll learn, thought Davy. The rockets in the valley made a double echo thud with pressure waves inside the aircraft. They were 200 feet out and now and slowed to 60 knots. Davy could finally see the hole in the jungle that was to be their LZ. Davy felt the aircraft take its first hit and Bob and Vick opened up on the M-60's.

"Taking fire at 3 o'clock."

Instantaneously the 3 o'clock position (directly on the right hand side of the Huey) exploded as a pair of 17-pound rockets impacted. Fifty feet out now and airspeed down to 20 knots. Davy could finally see fully down into the LZ. He brought the aircraft gently to a hover over the top.

"Torque stabilized at 37 pounds," said the co-pilot.

The trees were taller than he thought, maybe 75 to 100 feet and layers of foliage all the way down. Davy could see the mini guns from the breaking Cobras raking the area 20 meters to his front. It sounded like his Sanyo fan at base camp on high speed. He could hear small arms fire all around him. The team wasn't in the LZ, but must be near, maybe in the tree line; however still engaged. The LZ looked too small. Damn, he thought. I don't want to use the strings. Davy keyed his intercom.

"Bob, can we get in there?"

"Maybe low enough to use the ladders," came the immediate reply.

"Okay." Davy started down.

"Clear down left."

"Move left two feet."

"Clear left two feet."

"Move tail right one foot."

"Tail clear right one foot."

The crew was barking instructions above the roar of their M-60's as they screwed themselves down into the hole. As they descended, Davy smelled rotting vegetation and cordite. The mixture to choked him. It grew darker as they went deeper.

Davy could feel sporadic hits to the aircraft, but no major damage yet.

"Forward two feet."

Davy had kept the aircraft main rotor blades at the forward edge of clearance from the start. "Can't do it," said Davy. "Then that's it," said Bob, "We'll have to use the strings." They were still forty feet off the ground and out of clearance. Davy looked again at the trees and vegetation to his front. It was green with no large limbs or dead hardwood. He moved forward two feet and watched the blades eat into the trees.

"Clear down left."

"Clear down right."

The crew continued instruction as they chopped their way down. The Cobras continued to work both sides of the LZ with rockets and mini guns.

They made it all the way down to 6 feet before the lowest layer of vegetation stopped them. They were still too high for the team to get on. Shit, we'll have to use the ladders, thought Davy. He knew that would be another one to two minutes exposure time while the team climbed, and worse, they couldn't shoot for suppression while they climbed. Davy keyed the intercom. "Drop the ladders." The M-60's immediately fell silent as the crew scrambled forward to kick the ladders out. Five seconds later, the M-60's came to life. The ladders were out.

Davy could hear weapons all around him, but he still could not see anything. He was concentrating on keeping the helicopter at an absolutely stationary hover. "They're coming now," Bob shouted over the intercom.

When the ladders had come out, the team started to move toward the helicopter. They had been at the northeast corner of the LZ in a tree line at about the eight o'clock position to the ship. They moved the ten yards to the helicopter crouched, walking backwards, and firing as they went. Davy still could not see them or the enemy, but he could feel the aircraft being pounded by hits.

" They're only seven of them," Bob said over the intercom.

"Okay," responded Davy, "Get them all on. We'll take them all out."

It would be a max load for a hover hole, thought Davy, but it would save having to send a second bird in there. He also knew there was no other option; to split the team would ensure the death of those left to wait.

As they backed up toward the helicopter, one team member dropped to his knees, clutched his Car-15 to his chest and slowly rolled forward. The others kept firing and backing to the helicopter. They reached the left ladder and three of the remaining six passed underneath the tail boom to the right ladder. The three on the left continued to fire util they saw the three on the right reach the ladder. They had been trained to balance loads and they did so instinctively. Only when the others had reached the right ladder did the first man on each side stop firing his weapon and begin climbing.

Davy could feel them on the ladders by the shifting center of gravity and the necessary increase in hover power. He also heard their rifles fall silent. Time seemed to have stopped. The 30 seconds it took for the team to reach the ladders seemed like 30 years.

As the team climbed, the hail of bullets steadily increased. Davy could smell JP-4, which meant the fuel cells had been hit. Vic keyed the intercom.

"I've been hit."

The bullet had entered his left groin. There was no exit wound. Davy could hear his machine gun still firing.

Bob keyed his mike. "Okay, they're all on the ladders. Get us out of here Davy."

Ladder extraction of Recon Team

As he started to raise the collective pitch, Davy saw his first enemy soldier that day. He came running from the bushes and stopped ten feet to Davy's left front, put his rifle to his shoulder, and drew a careful bead at Davy. Davy meant to key the intercom, but he squeezed through the first indent to the UHF transmit position.

"Bob, kill the bastard at 11 o'clock. 11 o'clock."

Davy watched the M-60's tracers move over quickly towards the enemy soldier. Just as the tracers began to rip across his abdomen, the soldier fired. Although he was looking directly at him, Davy did not see the enemy soldier fire. The large Plexiglas windshield just exploded, showering the cockpit with fragments.

Three bullets hit Davy with sledgehammer impacts. The first hit the top center of his chest armor, the second slightly to the left on the armor, and the third went through his left arm and entered his chest. The force of the first two bullets was spread over his upper body by the chicken plate. It knocked the air from his lungs. The force also broke the left seat runner and allowed the armored seat to slide back 6 inches on the broken side. Even as the seat jumped back, Davy instinctively extended his right arm on the stick to maintain position.

More enemy soldiers closed in on the aircraft and a volume of hits steadily increased.

Davy keyed the intercom to tell the co-pilot he was hit and to take the aircraft. He found he couldn't talk, that he couldn't even bring air into his lungs.

Vic's machine gun fell silent. With the loss of suppressive fire on the right, the enemy's fire became even heavier. Bursts now ripped into the helicopter from every angle. The man first on the right ladder made it in and immediately laid down in the cargo area.

Another burst came through the cockpit, this time from the right tearing through the instrument panel and radio compartment. The lights for all the warning systems flashed crazily on and off, then went out. Davy had managed to force a breath in and again keyed the intercom. The intercom and radio system were dead. Davy was bleeding heavily from his arm and needed to turn the controls over to the co-pilot so he could put pressure on the injury and stop the flow. He looked over to the co-pilot and started to yell and then stopped. The co-pilot was slumped forward, hanging from his straps. His helmet had been spun around by a bullet impact so that the earpiece was to the front. The front of his flight suit was covered with blood dripping from his helmet.

The second man on the right ladder stood straight up as if coming to attention and fell backwards. The first troop on the left, as he reached the top of the ladder, also tumbled off. The next troop on the left scampered up the rocking ladder and into the cargo area. The two remaining team members at the bottom of the ladders had stopped climbing and were simply hunched up clinching the rungs. They knew the helicopter should have been moving up by now.

Davy's left arm was numb. He could still feel the collective pitch in his hand, but he couldn't move his arm. He looked down to the collective pitch and saw the flowing river of blood running down his arm onto the collective and pooling on the floor. Without raising the collective lever, they could not climb. At least if we get out of the hole, thought Davy, we can get away from the enemy fire. Davy tried again – nothing. The bone and muscle had been shot away. Davy also knew that without the intercom and course guidance to get out of the hole from the crew, they were probably going to hit a tree with their tail rotor, spin and crash. Davy rolled his whole body to the right in the seat and the collective came up. The movement was far too much. The helicopter shot up.

As the helicopter rose, the enemy troops closed into the LZ and were firing vertically into the belly. Davy moved the helicopter forward another foot as they ascended rapidly, chopping even further into the trees than on the way in. Better than the tail rotor, he thought.

At sixty feet, the main rotor struck a tree trunk severing six inches from one of the main rotor blades behind the main spar in the area of the honeycomb. The helicopter shuddered and picked up a severe lateral vibration, but the main spar held and the aircraft continued to climb.

As they cleared the trees, the team member on the left ladder fell free.

Davy waited until the ladders were clear, then added forward stick to gain airspeed. All was quiet now as they climbed to the north except for the eerie whistling wail from the main rotor where the blade skin had been peeled back from the honeycomb on the blade strike.

The troop on the right ladder dangled lifelessly from where he had attached himself to the rung by his stabo rig and d-snap rings.

"Bob, Bob," Davy yelled. "Oh, my God, Bob please come and help me." As he turned and looked back into the cargo area, he saw the two team members on the floor riddled with bullets. The sound proofing that covered the roof was shredded as if by a razor and blowing in the wind.

Then he saw Vic. The top of his body was extending into the cargo area from the gunner's well and his eyes were open with a fixed stare. "Bob, Bob," he screamed.

He had to turn around to the other shoulder to see into the crew chief's well. He turned and saw Bob in a half-standing position laying over his machine gun. His body was covered with multiple wounds.

"Oh God, no Oh God, please no."

Davy just let the helicopter fly as it was still climbing and headed East. He was cold and knew he couldn't last much longer due to loss of blood. He had to set it down. He saw a large open area to his front and held the cyclic with his knees while using his right hand to lower the collective and start down at about a 10 degree angle. He was sure that he was still in Laos and had not crossed the

Ho Chi Minh trail yet, but it made no difference. He had to get the aircraft on the ground now.

He flew with his right arm and allowed the aircraft to simply impact the ground without slowing his descent. Davy remembers the skids collapsing and then waking up in the evacuation hospital in Pleiku. He was told that the Panthers and his chase aircraft had been right behind him all the way from the LZ to the crash landing site and immediately landed next to his aircraft. Unfortunately, there were no other surviving crewmembers or recon team members. After they recovered all the bodies and weapons, they pulled the crypto gear from the nose compartment and Spad 01 dropped a 500 lb bomb directly on the top of the aircraft, leaving only a hole in the ground.

Davy was medevaced to Japan for a series of operations on his left arm and shoulder and then medevaced again to Fort MacArthur, California. Fort MacArthur, in San Pedro was quite near his mother's home in Torrance and she was able to come and visit him frequently until he was finally medically discharged from the Army.

CHAPTER 15 Confession

On August 14, 1992 a middle-aged man of about 45 years of age enters the confessional at Saint Lawrence Martyr Church. He sits and tells his Father Confessor, "Forgive me Father for I have sinned." The priest answers, "Yes, I know that my brother" and makes the sign of the cross. "I know of your sin- I know it because I was here and you were not- you missed mass on Sunday."

"Yes Father"

"Any other sins?

"No Father"

"Three Hail Mary's and an Our Father"

"The Lord has freed you from your sins. Go in peace"

The penitent responds, "Thanks be to God."

Both men exit the confessional and stroll toward the church doors. The former penitent says, "Hey, it's still early, let's go catch some waves."

The Priest smiles and immediately says, "You bet- throw your board in the back and we'll head to Torrance Beach."

They walk out to the parking lot to an old VW van and Davy opens the driver's door, gets in and removes his Roman collar and places it on the tray under the dash. He unbuttons his shirt. He has his swimming trunks in the back and will finish changing at the beach.

Will pops open the swing-up door at the back of the bus and loads his board, trunks and wet suit.

They turn right on Pacific Coast Highway. Davy says, "I'm glad you are back and living over at mom's. It was hard on her when Grandpa and then Grandmother passed on."

"I'm just glad I can be of help to her and I am happy to be there. And I think she is happy to have me there," replied Will. Will had spent the last 20 years in federal prison. Will said, "It is hard to believe all the turmoil and craziness that we went through since we left that house on Reynolds just to get here again- on our way to go surfing like we did when we left the house back then."

"I love you brother", said Davy.

"I have always known that. And I you", said Will. "But I still think a lot about an appointment I made a long time ago with a friend of mine named Max."

AFTERWORD as of 2020:

Will Davis returned to college at the age of 45 at California State College at Dominguez Hills near Torrance. He graduated with a degree in history and obtained his secondary school teaching credentials and is still teaching history at Torrance High School at the age of 71 years of age, but will retire at the end of this school year. He has been married to the former Linda Solem since 2001. They live at the family house on Reynolds Drive in Torrance. His and Davy's mother passed away in 1999. Will cared for her during her declining years. He does not give interviews nor discuss his activities in the 1960's or 1970's. He still has nightmares of meeting with Max as he moves nearer to death, but has decided that he must accept God's forgiveness- only the sin of self-centered pride makes a person think that their sins are beyond His reach. Will has surrendered to his fate and is relaxed with God's ultimate decision. Will and Linda attend St. Lawrence Martyr Church each Sunday. Davy comes over for dinner every Saturday if he is in town.

Father Davis retired from the priesthood at age 69 after serving in several locations across the U.S. He now spends most of his time fundraising for, and supporting, the Vinh Son Orphanage in Kontum, Vietnam. He had been introduced to the Orphanage when he served in Kontum and has since returned several times to visit and discover their needs[21]. He loved flying Hueys and often dreams of flying smooth as silk over green lush fields and swooping up and down the mountains and valleys as if by magic. He also enjoyed surfing for many years after his left arm healed, although he never fully recovered the full use of the arm. He hopes to return to surfing as soon as he recovers from hip replacement surgery. And although the young surfers call him "the old man" and make fun of his big board, they all give way to him when he wants a wave and know somehow that he is a very special person.

---

[21] Although this is a novel and therefore a story of fiction, the Vinh Son Orphanage is very real and needs funding to provide shelter, food and medical care for the orphans of the Central Highlands. If you can help, please contact the Friends of Vinh Son Orphanage (FVSO), P.O. Box9322-C, Auburn, CA 95604-9322. Website is: FriendsofVSO.org
Email at: FriendsofVSO@gmail.com